MURDER IN CITY HALL

A Plot Twist Cozy Mystery

Massachusetts Cozy Mystery
Book 3

ANDREA KRESS

© 2023

Created with Vellum

Chapter 1

The department directors had come into the meeting early knowing that the Mayor was a stickler for punctuality. No indication had been given about the nature of the assembly, but because it was on short notice, it was assumed that something of importance had occurred. Looks were exchanged among the men, for there were no female department directors, and a few tugged at their shirt collars or smoothed their hair as they waited. The big clock on the wall told them that they had five more minutes to wait. Their instincts told them it would be wise not to chatter during that time.

Finally, the door at the front of the room opened and the Mayor strode through at a measured pace, looking down his long nose at the group that rose to its feet. Behind him Henry Rogers, his assistant and smaller shadow, followed with a stern look on his face. The Mayor stood behind the podium, took out a small piece of paper and laid it before him. He motioned to the crowd to be seated, waited until the room was entirely quiet before leaning one arm on the podium in a familiar gesture, and scowled.

"Gentlemen." He paused. "If there's one thing I can't stand, it's dishonesty." He scanned the faces of the men seated before him. Henry stood off to the side with his hands crossed in front of him, his posture at ease but eyes alert as he looked at the crowd.

"Dishonesty. It breeds mistrust. We all like to trust each other, don't we? And if all of you wish to be in this room in the future, you've got to have the trust of the people." There were some sidelong glances given among the men seated before him and a few looked down at the hands in their lap.

"What am I talking about?" The Mayor gave a chuckle. "Oh, I think you know. It's probably not you and probably not your deputy directors who are to blame. They're too busy shuffling papers on their desks to see what's going on around them. It's the men on the ground." He paused again and noticed that several in the audience looked at each other quizzically.

"Don't be so naïve, my friends. They're out on the street, issuing tickets, sometimes tearing them up first. They're taking an apple off the pushcart and nodding to the vendor. They're standing behind the counter waiting for the applicant, hemming and hawing about what the matter is until a little something passes across from one hand to another and suddenly everything is fine."

He paused again, stood back and pounded his fist on the podium. "It is not fine!"

That got their attention, and their eyes were wide and focused on the tall form of the Mayor, who now had a snarl on his face.

"It gives you a bad name. It gives the City of Boston a bad name. It gives me a bad name. And the last thing you want, or I want, is a bad name. Because the other thing that I can't stand is losing an election. If I lose an election, where do you think you will be?" He jerked his thumb over his shoulder in a vicious motion.

There were sideways glances in the audience and restless movements in the chairs.

"Understand?" He waited until they were still. "Now, go back to your departments, and tell the managers to tell the supervisors to tell their employees that this is a clean city! When I promised the voters that I would clean up Boston, I meant inside and outside. Not just those bootleggers and criminals preying on our people, but also those in our very midst who are nickel-and-diming citizens every day. Do I make myself clear?" he added with a shout.

"Yes, sir," they said to a man and stood up as he gave one last scowl and stalked away from the podium and out the door, trailed by Henry Rogers.

The men looked at one another in surprise and a hint accusation that suggested it was not their people who were perpetrating bribes, but those in some other department. The director of the department that oversaw boiler, mechanical safety, building permits and code inspections put on a bland expression although he suspected that some of his people were involved. He had a good idea who might be a likely culprit, but he had no idea that it would lead to murder.

Chapter 2

As the men were filing out of the meeting room, Amanda Burnside was driving past City Hall wondering how her former maid, Nora Gallagher, was enjoying her new job there. It seemed such a strange mode of thinking—most people didn't speak of work in terms of pleasure, but Amanda had come to find out that what many found to be drudgery was fulfilling for her. Of course, coming from a wealthy family in Beacon Hill, she was not digging ditches or scrubbing floors each day, which would be tedious, backbreaking and demoralizing. She had a job that utilized her organizational and interpersonal skills and benefitted the community: a rare combination for a woman.

The job was at first a volunteer effort at Mercy Hospital, part of her debutante community service experience. And while many of her friends from that group had moved on —a few to college, some to marry, others to spend their time socializing and waiting for marriage—she had continued at the hospital, mostly doing paperwork a few days a week. Mr. Barlow had come on as the new director within the past year, bringing new ideas and fresh energy and, recognizing a kindred spirit in Amanda, had offered her a part-time position refurbishing the Indigent Children's Clinic. The first task was renaming it the Children's Clinic. That morphed into extending clinic operations to the North End with the extensive help of Sons of Italy, and based on that success, he had just that morning proposed that she come on full time developing more clinics in the wider Boston area. Next on the agenda was looking into possible locations in the West End, a neighborhood with which she wasn't very familiar, at least in terms of what would make a good place for that purpose.

Other young women might have been daydreaming about boyfriends, fiancés or marriage, but she was buoyed by the knowledge that her ability and resourcefulness were recognized and now rewarded. Her only obstacle at that point was convincing her parents that her acceptance of the job was a good thing, not an obstacle to finding a partner in life. Although they had some good reasons, it was a bit of a puzzle that her parents frowned on her younger sister, Louisa, being involved with a man, yet kept pushing Amanda towards a permanent relationship. One had been blossoming of late with Brendan Halloran, but she was taking that slowly.

The busy city streets gave way to the sedate and quiet Beacon Hill neighborhood with its brick homes and tall trees leafing out in the afternoon sunshine. Pulling the car into the garage in the back of the house, she went up the back stairs to the kitchen where Cook was clattering pans in preparation for dinner.

"Hello, Miss. You're home early."

"I wanted to be here when Louisa got back."

"She's home already," Simona, the new maid, said as she entered from the swinging door.

"There's ever so much luggage." Amanda had recommended her for the job to replace Nora after Louisa had left, so it was their first encounter. She probably wasn't aware that Louisa had been sent to Charleston with a friend and two chaperones to get her away from the nightclub owner who had become her boyfriend in Boston. A nice enough fellow, Amanda thought, but not someone her parents wanted their daughter to be associating with, much less dating.

Amanda went through the dining room, sitting room and up the stairs to see her sister, whose three-week exile had turned into six.

"Where's the pilgrim?" she called out.

Louisa put her head around the corner of her room and posed in the doorway, one hand extended up the doorway and the other on her hip.

"Oh, stop it, silly," Amanda said, giving her a warm hug. "You're not a movie star yet. Are you?"

"Alas, no. The next time I am sent into exile, I'll request Los Angeles and perhaps that will be my future calling."

"First of all, you'd better not pull any more stunts that get you sent away. And I should remind you that the typical outcast does not get to choose their destination."

"Spoilsport!"

"But just look at you! Abounding in health, rosy cheeks, no droopy looks."

Louisa reached around her neck and pulled a thin chain out from which hung a heavy ring and batted her eyelashes.

"What in the world is that?" Amanda asked.

"It's Beau's ring. Isn't it sweet?"

"While you wrote as Daddy instructed and called every Sunday, somehow the name Beau was never mentioned. Who the heck is he?" Amanda examined the ring. "Ha! A cadet at the Citadel. Just as I predicted."

"You did not," Louisa said petulantly as she put the ring back beneath the bodice of her dress.

"Who else knows about this?"

"Very few people, of course. Our little secret. Well, Eunice knows since she's the one who made the introductions at the dance."

Amanda pushed the jumble of her sister's clothes on the bed aside to sit down. "The dance? It seems you left out a lot of details in your letters and calls home."

"The cadets host a dance every month with a different club or debutante group and Eunice's cousin belongs to an elite social group. Top drawer in Charleston."

Amanda scowled at Louisa's new phrase. "Are there groups who are considered lower drawer or middle drawer?" she teased.

Louisa breezed on. "It was a very glamorous setting at the Citadel: the cadets in their uniforms and impeccable manners and a lovely dance band. Old-fashioned and sedate, naturally, but it gave the opportunity to have an actual conversation with one's partner." She sighed and picked up a crumpled dress from the pile on the bed and tossed it onto a chair. "Needs cleaning. And who's the new maid? What happened to Nora?"

"Simona is her name. She's very good. Her parents own a restaurant in the North End and, though she was helping them out, she was looking for a paying position. While Nora was working here, she took a secretarial course and then got herself a job at City Hall."

"Well! Ambitious young thing. And I'm glad we now know people in high places."

"As her replacement, Simona is working out well, thank you. I saw Nora the other day and, because she is only a secretary, people seem to think that she doesn't exist. Which means she observes the most interesting things in her new job."

"Such as?"

"The Mayor's stepson often comes breezing into the building, and some people think that he just comes in to get money from his father."

"Isn't that what a father is for?"

"Not every parent is as indulgent as Daddy is with you. She told me that the Mayor seems peeved about the situation."

"How old is he? A high school student?"

"No," Amanda laughed. "He's a young man in his twenties who, with his connections, should be gainfully employed. She said he's very cocky and sure of himself."

"I've seen him at the club. Kenny something, doesn't have the Mayor's last name. He can be a handful, from what I've heard."

"Now back to Beau. Tell me all about him."

"His name is Beauregard LeConte, and his family has been in Charleston for generations. Rice plantations or something although they have a gorgeous home in the city. I've even met his parents and they are lovely. He's in classes all the time so he couldn't show me their country place, but Eunice said it's spectacular."

"What does the ring mean?"

"As Beau put it, we are engaged to be engaged." She smiled and resumed sorting through her clothes.

"Wait a minute. What about Rob Worley? Does he know about this?"

"Of course not."

"Louisa, you do not seem the least bit concerned about carrying on with two men at the same time."

"Amanda. Honestly, you don't expect me to put all my eggs in one basket, do you? We'll just have to see what happens, that's all."

Her sister blinked in exasperation. "I'll bet that you have been writing Rob all along while waltzing with your cadet."

"Yes, so?"

"Rob has some good qualities although his choice of profession leaves something to be desired. However, and I never thought I would say this, you are being entirely callous and unfair to string him along while getting serious with another."

"Rob has been very attentive to me, but do you see a ring?" She held out her left hand to demonstrate its absence. The she opened her closet and began to hang up a dress.

"And there is something that I have been meaning to discuss with you," Amanda said, getting up from the bed. "Although I didn't want to put it in writing, and I couldn't talk to you on the phone with Mother and Daddy listening in." She moved past her sister and looked at the shoe boxes piled up. "To be clear, I was not snooping. I was merely perusing your wardrobe to select a gown for an evening out and needed appropriate shoes. As I shuffled through the boxes, I came across this." She found the box and opened it, revealing a stack of pieces of folded papers.

Louisa looked puzzled and took the box in her hands. "Oh, that. It's something that Rob asked me to hold onto for him."

"Do you know what these are?"

"Um, no." Louisa unfolded one and looked at it. "It says IOU, but I don't know what that means."

"In common parlance, it means, 'I owe you' and the amount is indicated along with a signature. It's a loan."

"Oh," Louisa said, putting the paper back in the box and resuming her fiddling with the clothes.

"It means that whoever the scribbler is who signed this borrowed money from Rob. Louisa, taken altogether, this is a huge amount of money. Why has Rob loaned this person so much money? There are other people in this stack, but this one stands out as being a significant debtor. Do you think this person holds something over Rob so that he can't refuse to loan him money?"

"Gosh, I don't know. I didn't think about it. And I don't even know who it is."

"What it means is that he has put himself in a vulnerable position since the borrower might get desperate and attempt to take them back. And worse, he had put you and our family in a vulnerable position. What if the scribbler decides not to pay Rob back but instead destroy the evidence? The debt would be erased. What if he knows this is here in this house, in your bedroom? He might try to break in and steal it. He could set fire to our house to destroy the evidence. Why did you allow Rob to endanger us all?"

Louisa finally understood the implications of what her sister was suggesting.

"That's a horrible suggestion."

"But it could happen."

"I had no idea! What should I do?"

"I have a few suggestions," Amanda said.

Chapter 3

The cause of the Mayor's tirade against his employees was due to a certain Inspector Kehoe who was tasked with responding to building code violations. However, the day before he had been busy plying his specialty: bilking the unaware homeowner or landlord. He had several different approaches that he used. For a simple violation, once meeting with the potential target, he would tilt his hat back on his head, rub his chin and look pensive. If the person was not outright aggressive, the victim usually took a path of rebuttal.

The most common initial excuse given was ignorance of the law, which everyone knew was no excuse. Inspector Kehoe had no reaction. Then came counter accusations about the neighbor who they were sure was responsible for having called in the violation. Again, the inspector kept a straight face. This was followed by the weaker contention that the law itself was ridiculous and should be changed. Inspector Kehoe listened respectfully to this litany of diminishing arguments in silence. He waited for the inevitable, "What happens now?"

The inspector had done this dance with so many others, he was practiced in his excruciatingly slow response. That kept the suspect, in this case a homeowner named Mr. Brown, who had popped home for a bite of lunch, in suspense imagining at the least he would get a ticket and a fine and at the worst go to jail for not fixing a broken sidewalk. But still Inspector Kehoe did not speak but walked around the offending piece of concrete, poked at it with the tip of his boot and shook his head.

"Someone could trip and break their neck," was all he said.

"It was like this when I bought the house," was a familiar response, and Mr. Brown used it. Blame it on the former owner.

"Just think of the cost of having to resolve a lawsuit if somebody was seriously injured."

"Nobody's ever mentioned it before."

"If you're handy with construction materials," which he knew the man was not by looking at his pristine suit and shiny shoes, "you could fix it yourself over the weekend. Otherwise…."

The befuddled Mr. Brown looked back to the porch where his wife stood, holding their baby and looking concerned because she could not hear the conversation. "I might be able to find someone to break this up and redo it," he said tentatively.

"That's good to hear. I'm guessing you have the tools. But are you aware of the specs for public sidewalks—making sure of the grade of cement, the curing time, the dimensions, and so forth?"

The man's shoulders slumped. "Of course not. I work in an office."

Kehoe shook his head and proceeded to take his ticket book out of his back pocket.

"Isn't there some way we can clear this up?" the man asked.

"I could recommend someone to do the work. It wouldn't be too expensive."

The man reached in his pocket and pulled out a ten-dollar bill and held it discreetly in his hand so only the inspector could see it.

Kehoe looked away. "I'm sure the work would cost at least twenty dollars, if not more."

The man shrugged and reached in his pocket again. Kehoe stopped him with a look.

"The work needs to be done. If your neighbor called it in, they are not going to stop because I walk away. They'll call it in again, only a different inspector may come out and then you'll be in the soup."

"Okay, why don't you give me the information and I'll arrange to have it fixed."

It was the more complicated solution, but Inspector Kehoe had no intention of getting his brother-in-law out to do the work for a mere twenty dollars. It might cost at least twice that. He dug in his pockets and sifted through several business cards until he came to one, squinted at it, turned it over and his eyebrows went up.

"I think this guy does cement work."

"Thank you. So, can we consider this only a warning and once I get it repaired, that's that?" the man asked.

"Sure, sure. We have better things to do than bother people about these minor issues. Although someone could have tripped and got badly hurt. You still might be liable for any damages if you don't deal with it immediately." What he didn't mention was that the sidewalk was City property, and the homeowner was not responsible for its repair nor any injury as a result.

"I'll be sure to get right on it," the man said and shook Kehoe's hand gratefully. He went back to the porch and faced his wife, who had many questions about the interaction. What the inspector didn't notice was that the mother-in-law peering from behind a second-story window.

This was a routine day for Inspector Kehoe and he had handed out several citations, made some cash and a few jobs. But still, he wanted more.

AT THE END of the week, Kehoe counted his take. It was good, but there had to be some way to make more money. He drove over to the coffee shop just outside of downtown where many of the inspectors gathered either at the beginning or the end of the day. The only one there was Rick Slater, who waved him over to the counter where he sat.

"Coffee for my good man," he said to the waitress as a way of ordering for him, although he had no intention of paying for it himself. "How's business?"

"Hard day today. Cranky homeowners who need to argue about every little thing."

"Don't I know it," Slater said as the waitress put a cup of coffee in front of Kehoe.

"Pie? Doughnut?" she asked, but he shook his head.

"*Cheapskates,*" she thought.

They sipped without speaking for a few minutes.

"Who's that kid I saw you with in your truck the other day?" Kehoe said casually.

"He's my sister's kid. I was giving him a ride back home."

"Watch out about that. I gave my girlfriend a ride one day and our conscientious colleague, Inspector Torgan, took me aside in his holy-pious way to tell me it was against the rules."

Slater scoffed. "He's got the whole rule book memorized. Did you ever see such a neat desk? I see him wipe it down every Friday before he leaves work."

"Are you kidding?"

"I'm not. So, I put a dusting of sugar on it after he left." He sniggered.

"So that's where all the ants came from!" Kehoe laughed.

"If they put us in a decent place instead of the basement of City Hall, we wouldn't be invaded by 'vermin,' as the boss refers to them."

Kehoe held his coffee cup up to his lips and paused in thought. "That always confuses me. I thought vermin meant an animal, not a bug."

Slater shrugged. "Maybe you mean varmint?"

"Maybe. Anyhow, how's that side business you've got going?"

"What side business?"

"Clearing out houses."

"Who told you that?"

Kehoe waved his hand away. "Not important. I'm a bit short of cash just now. I'm always ready to lend a hand."

Slater glared at him. "There's scarcely enough business for me. An hour or two on the weekend."

"That's not what I hear. I've got a friend who works upstairs at City Hall who says he sees you up there talking to some woman a couple of times a week."

"So? Maybe we're stepping out."

"She may think so, but I think you've got a sweet deal going on somehow. She's the lady who has something to do with finances. Always a good person to know." He winked then looked at the clock on the wall. "Better get back to clock out for the day." He patted Slater on the shoulder and smiled. "Thanks for the joe."

The waitress appeared and stood in front of Slater, waiting for him to pay, while his co-worker sauntered out the door. He put the exact change on the counter, swiveled off the chair and made to leave.

"Thanks, chump," she muttered.

Slater hurried to his truck and decided to follow closely behind Kehoe and nudged his bumper every time they had to stop. Slater had a hard time keeping a straight face as

Kehoe was sticking his head out of the window and yelling back at him. He loved playing the dumb clown and bumped the back of the other man's truck several times more, being careful not to be so rough as to leave a dent in the bumper. He deserved it, trying to horn in on his racket. By the time they got back to City Hall, Kehoe was almost purple in the face.

"What the hell—," he began, storming out of his truck, intending to sock the other man in the jaw before he saw their boss waiting for them and held back.

"Just the guy I was looking for," the boss said. He led the way into the building and hit the elevator button for the basement floor. Just as the doors were closing, Slater pushed his way through the closing doors.

"Top of the evening to you," he said to his boss, a smarmy smile on his face at the obvious discomfort of the other two men.

They rode in silence although Kehoe was sure that Slater was stifling a giggle. The doors opened and Slater gestured with his hand that the others should exit before him. They walked down the hall to the bullpen, as the inspectors called the open area with small desks where they could write up the day's work.

The boss went into his office, which had a spacious desk and padded chair and intentionally no other available seating since there were stacks of papers on the other two chairs. Kehoe stood before the desk while the boss looked him over.

"I got a call today. A woman out on Chestnut Street. That's your patch, isn't it?" he asked unnecessarily, turning to look at a map of the city with the inspectors' areas marked out. He knew it by heart but liked to see the inspector squirm as he paused to draw his finger over the area.

"Yes, sir."

"She said that you were trying to put the squeeze on them yesterday."

Kehoe looked puzzled. "I didn't talk to any woman on Chestnut Street." He thought of the young woman with the baby on the porch. There was no way she would have called in about the conversation he had with her husband. She had been too far away to overhear and he was probably too embarrassed about the situation in the first place to give her the details.

"Name of Brown?" Kehoe asked.

"Nah. The old lady. The mother-in-law. She's lived there for ages. Her daughter and son-in-law live with her. She's been a precinct captain for years among other things and she knows the score. She figured that you tried to scare the guy into getting the sidewalk fixed, refused a bribe, and instead shuttled him over to your brother-in-law to do the work and soak him for more."

"I did?" He reached into his pocket and pulled out a small stack of business cards and looked puzzled at the accusation. "Guys in the trades give me these all the time. I'm just trying to be helpful. Trying to save the taxpayer the expense of going through a ticket and a citation—you know how upset people get about that. Not to mention a court appearance if they get testy and decide to contest it. You told us you didn't want us spending all our time hanging out at court, cooling our heels waiting for our cases to come up."

"I know what I told you! But I didn't tell you to refer the repair business to anybody. Much less to your extended family. That old bag has been around long enough to know every trick in the book. So cut it out! The Mayor got on every director of every department in the City today and chewed us out about having a clean city. That doesn't just mean no gangsters, gambling or bootlegging. It means not fleecing the public about unnecessary repairs that you and your family overcharge them for."

The inspector let the boss cool down for a few moments before saying simply, "Yes, sir."

"And don't think that just because you hobnob with the Mayor's stepson that you're protected. Now, get out!"

Kehoe nodded his head and left as quickly as he could, glad that he wasn't threatened with being fired although that could well be the next step if he weren't careful. A few feet away from the boss's door was Inspector Torgan, who had evidently heard the conversation. His usual solemn face looked sad, and Kehoe was having none of it.

"Do you always listen at doors?" he asked. "Isn't there some commandment about that?"

"It wasn't intentional. But if you want to talk sometime, brother, the word of God can be soothing and healing."

Kehoe shot him a dirty look. "Are you trying to preach to me? Get lost."

He strode back to his desk, aware that the entire room full of inspectors had also overheard the scolding from the boss and the subsequent comment from Torgan. Rather than look abashed or repentant, he made a face and strutted to his desk, getting a big laugh from his fellow employees. Bravado was important.

The boss had come to the threshold of his office and stood silently until the laughter died down and Kehoe turned to see what everyone was looking at. No words were exchanged, but he went back to his desk and made himself look busy.

Chapter 4

The building inspection team wasn't the only one where word of the Mayor's speech about dishonesty had filtered down. The Police Chief had taken those comments personally since the Mayor had used the phrase 'taking the apple off the cart,' a comment that anyone would know from personal observation or watching a movie was a reference to a beat cop. The Chief knew his was one of the few departments that issued tickets as well, also referenced in the speech, a prime opportunity to wield power over the public. The fact that he felt the Mayor was addressing his remarks to him personally made him even more eager to talk to his folks and lower the boom.

While the Mayor had assembled the directors in a room with seating, the Chief called for his senior staff to stand on Friday morning as they met in the wide hall outside his office after shooing away any secretaries and making sure that the doors to offices were closed. The implied secrecy of the assembly was unnerving, and Brendan Halloran, who represented the detective division and was unaware of the Mayor's speech, wondered what was going on. Were there going to be layoffs or budget cuts, or was the Chief going to resign? What he wasn't expecting was a lecture about honesty, trust and tarnishing the reputation of the force. And unlike the Mayor's harangue that didn't identify to which department he was referring, the Chief pointed his finger around the room as he spoke. The staff members gathered were unsettled by the ferocious manner he used, so unlike the usual sly delivery he gave, and he ended his tirade with, "Get back to work!"

When Halloran got back to the detectives' area, the others stopped him before he went into his office.

"What's going on?" Dominick Barone asked.

Halloran considered how best to handle the situation and faced the group in the bullpen.

"I understand the Mayor chewed out the department directors, and the Chief in turn lectured us about integrity, honesty and, frankly, not taking bribes."

"Why now?" someone asked. "What's going on?"

Halloran shrugged his shoulders. "Someone must have called the Mayor's office." They looked at each other. "It wasn't one of us, or we would have had the hammer come down on us already. But you know how the Mayor is about staying Mayor."

That garnered a grim chuckle, but Halloran was serious. "Don't ever, ever give anyone the advantage in thinking you are on the take. Do not, repeat, do not take an apple off a cart, a sawbuck from a speeder or a smile from a young woman to fix a ticket. Someone is watching very closely and in times like these, where we all value our jobs, we do not want to put them in jeopardy." He went into his office and Dominick appeared a few minutes later.

"Are we in trouble here?"

"I don't think so. It's some other City employees on the street that they're worried about. Driving around unsupervised. Maybe someone's been doing a shakedown and the victim got fed up, I don't know." He shuffled through a pile of phone messages.

"Why does that apply to us? Does he think we rifle through a dead guy's pockets for chump change or something?"

Halloran looked up. "It's been done before. Believe me."

Dominick shuddered. "That's disgusting."

"Yes, and for some folks, profitable."

Dominick hesitated and looked around. "You've got the office here, but when is the Chief going to announce that you are the boss?"

"I have no idea," Halloran responded, not looking up. "Maybe he wants to keep me on tenterhooks."

"That sounds like the Chief." After a pause he asked, "What have you got going this weekend?"

Halloran looked up. "Amanda is coming to dinner at my folks' place."

"Whoa!"

Halloran gave him a withering look. "What?"

"Serious, huh?"

"Don't you have some paperwork to attend to?" he asked in response.

"Sure thing," Dominick responded, edging to the door. "Boss."

Halloran threw a pencil at his retreating back.

If Dominick thought Brendan Halloran was nervous about the dinner, he was right. He felt like an idiot, having blurted out the invitation to her in the first place without consulting his parents although that bridge had subsequently been crossed. His mother was exuberant, which threw him a bit. It wasn't as if he hadn't introduced previous girlfriends to his family, but she was taking this as if the Queen of England was dropping by for tea.

"Oh, what shall I make?" his mother had begun, pinching her lower lip between her fingers. "How fancy should it be?"

"Seven courses would be fine," he had said. She batted him on the arm.

"What do you think she would like?'

"I have no idea," he said.

"How can you have no idea if you've been seeing the young lady for some time. Eating meals and so forth. What does she like to eat?"

"Judging from my experience, she is quite fond of Italian food."

"What? I don't know how to make any of that."

"I'm talking about our experience having meals. They were all in the North End at Catalano's, which is Italian. We have never discussed what she eats at home."

"So, you've never been to her house for a meal?"

"Not yet."

"Where are her people from?"

"Beacon Hill."

"Oh, my," his mother responded. "Roast chicken would be nice," she said after a few moments.

"Okay, Ma, I've got to go," he had said and dashed out before she plagued him with the infinite details of the meal. Since it would be Sunday, his brother Patrick, the priest, would be in attendance, along with his sister, her husband, baby Imogen, and his younger brother and sister. Might as well throw Amanda into the deep end and see if she could swim.

Chapter 5

Halloran was nervous as he approached her house in Beacon Hill. He had met her parents many times, but suddenly this date had taken on more significance. Simona answered the door when he rang, and he was ushered into an empty sitting room.

"Are the Burnsides at home?" he asked.

"They're still at church," she replied. "I'll get Miss Amanda," she said, going up the staircase. He stood looking at an oil painting of an old-fashioned ship with full sails.

"That's the famous ship that started the family fortune," Amanda said, observing him as she came down the stairs.

"Lucky you." He smiled at her. "Why aren't you at church?"

"Mother and Daddy decided to go to a later service today, and, of course, I had a previous engagement." She had on a blue dress that matched the color of her eyes and its skirt swirled around her slim legs.

"You look lovely. As usual."

She wrinkled her nose at him, deflecting the compliment. "As usual? Don't I ever surpass my usual loveliness?"

"I'd have to say that low-backed, dark blue evening gown was pretty special."

"Our first kiss."

"Not the last," he said, leaning over to kiss her on the cheek. "Had to get that one in before we get to my parents and the chaos begins." She gave him a puzzled look as he helped her into her coat, then she stepped to the mirror in the foyer to put on her hat.

"No time like the present," she said, taking a deep breath.

As he drove, she realized she had never asked him where his family lived, and she didn't want to jump to conclusions and assume it was Dorchester.

"Why do you say chaos?"

"Just joking. My sister, Bridie, and her husband, Frank, live with my parents. They have baby Imogen who is either teething, experiencing colic or just plain cranky. Sometimes it's noisy."

"I can't remember a baby in our house. I seem to have blocked out Louisa's early existence entirely."

"That explains some things," he laughed. "She's quite a handful."

"She wasn't always that way. I always thought of her as shy and timid and then something happened."

"Rob Worley?"

"He noticed her first when his band was hired to be at her coming-out party."

"The Valentine Ball. Who could forget?" He smiled, remembering that was when they first met.

"It was as if a switch flipped when an older, sophisticated man paid attention to her. She suddenly had confidence. Which soon became daring. That evolved into recklessness. I don't think I told you that some charming Southern boy gave her a ring when she was in Charleston."

Halloran looked over at her when the car was stopped at a light. "Does Worley know?"

She shrugged.

"Engaged?"

"This is strange. She explained it as 'engaged to be engaged,' whatever that means."

"Do your parents know?"

"Of course not. Once again, I am called on to cover for her antics. It's getting tiresome."

"You don't have to, you know."

She didn't respond.

"You said that you were coming into some money soon and might look for an apartment. That could give you the space to detach from her escapades."

"The problem with that idea is that she would try to finagle her way into being my roommate, which would be worse. Although she does have a spectacular evening wardrobe of which I could avail myself."

"Bad idea. Instead of your parents worrying about her, it would fall entirely on your shoulders. I think she would take tremendous advantage of the situation."

"True. But I haven't decided about getting an apartment yet. Now that work is full time, how will I find a moment to look around for one, much less furnish it?"

"You'd be surprised to know there are plenty of furnished places for rent. In my case, I got the family's old furniture, so it looks like some eighty-year-old man lives there. It might prevent some villain from breaking and entering, at least."

"Here we are," he said, pulling up in front of a two-story clapboard in Brookline.

"It's lovely," Amanda said, admiring the front yard with its beech trees' long branches arching out over the lawn. She saw daffodils peeping out from the leaves near the bushes at the front door and wondered about the gardens in the backyard.

He opened the car door for her and said, "We've only been here about five years, and my father can't stop thinking of new projects to make it bigger or more modern."

"I don't think I ever asked you, but what kind of work does your father do?"

"He and my uncle own a construction company and a separate printing company."

Amanda was puzzled as these seemed very different in nature.

"I'll explain later." He opened the door to a large living room with several seating areas and a great deal of talking from some adjoining areas, piano practicing through a room to the right and a baby fussing from an upper room. "See what I meant by chaos?" he said.

Amanda thought it all sounded cheerful but also very noisy compared to her sedate home.

Brendan took their coats and put them in a closet by the front door and then led her to the back of the room from which the voices emanated. As soon as they got to the doorway from the living room into a vast dining room, someone yelled, "There they are!" And they were swarmed by so many people, hugging, patting and asking questions.

"Everyone, this is Amanda Burnside. My mother and father," he began.

His mother was small although she and her son shared the same pale skin, dark hair and intense blue eyes. She beamed at Amanda and her handshake was warm. His father was considerably taller, broad chested and had red hair. Next was Angela, his teenage sister, then Frank, a tall blonde man, the brother-in-law.

"Angela, tell Sean to stop playing the piano. He's making the baby fuss."

"The baby fusses all the time," Frank said, watching her back as she went to do the chore. "I'll get Bridie," he added and left.

Amanda looked around the dining room at the dark wood of the breakfront stacked with dishes for the large family and the framed photos on the wall of elderly relatives in old-fashioned clothing. The table had been set for ten people with a highchair at one end, and she could smell roasted meat from the kitchen even behind the swinging door into the other room.

"Let me see how things are coming along," his mother said. "And where is Patrick?" The door swung open to a kitchen with what looked like a restaurant-gauge stove and ovens, sinks, two refrigerators, countertops and a long table with chairs where they might take their breakfast.

Are there more family members? Amanda thought. She hoped she could remember everyone's name.

"May I get you a glass of sacramental wine?" Mr. Halloran asked with a twinkle in his eye.

Amanda looked around and saw several cordial glasses with wine already poured and nodded her head; she was reassured that she wouldn't be the only one drinking or thought to be fast.

After handing her the glass, he led them into the living room where Angela appeared with the piano player, a gangly redhead like his father who shot over to Brendan and got him in a bear hug and received a light punch in the arm in return.

"This your girlfriend?" he asked cheekily, and Brendan made a fist as if to hit him again.

"I'm Amanda," she said and shook his hand.

"How did you two meet?" he asked.

"You're awfully forward," his father scolded mildly. "I expect we'll find out over dinner."

No sooner had they sat down on the comfortable sofa than the front door opened, and a tall, dark-haired priest entered the room.

"Patrick!" Mr. Halloran shouted. "Your mother's been worrying that you wouldn't get here."

They clapped each other on the back and the son said, "Sunday. Always busy, as you know. Back-to-back masses." He turned his attention to the sofa and Brendan stood and gave the priest a hug.

"This is my brother, Patrick. Father Halloran," he added with a serious face.

He held out his hand to Amanda, who was struck by the resemblance between the brothers although Patrick had a more serious look about him.

"Don't they feed you there?" his father asked, pointing to his lean frame.

"Nothing is as good as home cooking. Where's my sainted mother," he said in a faux brogue as he made his way through the dining room, presumably to the kitchen.

"I see everyone is having wine. How about it, Pop?" Sean asked.

"Milk is what is required for a growing boy," his father said.

"If I grow any more, I'll need new clothes and shoes and then you'll complain even more."

"This one's going to be a lawyer, for sure," Mr. Halloran said.

Frank came down the stairs followed by Bridie, a slightly taller version of her mother, holding a baby who was looking around at the talking adults.

Bridie was introduced and more than happy to plop the baby into Brendan's lap, to his surprise.

"What can you possibly see in this galoot?" she asked Amanda.

"This, by the way, is Imogen," Brendan said. The baby was only interested in his tie clip and tried to pull it off.

"Hello, dear," Amanda said and was met with huge brown eyes then a gummy grin.

"Here you go," Brendan said, holding the baby out to Amanda, who had never held an infant before.

"Let me put my glass down at least," she said, before taking up the child, who was much heavier than she imagined.

"Hello, you," she said, and the baby gazed into her eyes and smiled back when she smiled. Then Imogen's attention was caught by Amanda's necklace, which she grabbed and put in her mouth. Amanda laughed.

"Bridie, please. The infant will be eating the pearls in a minute," Brendan said, but it was Frank who picked up the little girl.

"Is she crawling yet?" Brendan asked.

It occurred to Amanda that she was clueless about the developmental stages of babies—when they teethed, talked, crawled or walked, but Brendan knew. Having so many siblings, it must have been inevitable that he would be familiar with it all.

"No, just rocking back and forth. Any day now. We can't wait until those teeth finally come through. She's been gnawing on everything."

"Come on, show me how you can crawl," Sean said, taking the baby and putting her on all fours on the carpet. She was frozen there for a moment and then fell back on her diapered bottom.

"I guess she's not going to perform on command," he said.

"She's a human, not a circus animal," Angela said. "Come here," and she picked up the baby, who was the fascinated by the crucifix on a chain that her young aunt wore. "Let's see what grandmother is doing in the kitchen." She took the child off through the dining room.

Brendan looked over to Amanda, raised his eyebrows and smiled as if to say, *I told you about the chaos.* She smiled in return, a bit overwhelmed by the number of people and trying to keep everyone straight. Just as she was tucking into her glass of wine, a gong sounded, and Mr. Halloran leapt to his feet.

"Dinner's ready," he said, holding out his arm to usher Amanda into the dining room. "Big house, lots of people, she needs to get everyone's attention somehow," he said, referring to the gong.

He escorted her to a place near the head of the table and motioned to his son. "Sit next to her, Brendan. Shield her from the hooligans."

Amanda smiled, not knowing how rowdy the meal might be as the rest of the family followed, with Mrs. Halloran coming in from the kitchen carrying a platter with two roast chickens on it. She sat opposite her husband and, looking toward her son, said, "Patrick?"

Everyone bowed their head, and he made the sign of the cross while everyone else did the same before saying a blessing on the family, the guest and the food. They crossed themselves again and Angela and Bridie got up to bring the side dishes in from the kitchen. The baby had a spoon in her hand and was banging on the highchair tray and looking very pleased with the noise she made.

"Oh, we've got a drummer now, too?" Mr. Halloran said.

"Maybe she could team up with Sean and start a dance band," Frank said.

"I was at a nightclub and that's exactly what the music sounded like," Brendan said.

Mr. Halloran stood up and carved the birds, his wife passed a bowl of mashed potatoes around the table in one direction while Bridie handed vegetables the other way. Frank picked up the breadbasket and offered it to Amanda, who, after taking out a Parker House roll, passed it to Brendan.

"You're getting the hang of this. You've got to act fast, or the food is gone in the blink of an eye."

"Who's been going to a nightclub?" his mother asked.

"It was for work," he responded with a wink at Amanda.

"I thought you were a police officer, not a talent scout," Sean said.

"Detective, my good man, detective."

"What's the difference?"

"I don't have to wear a uniform and the pay is much better."

"Patricia Curry said that her son is going to be a fireman and the department pays for their uniforms," his mother said.

"Why don't you be a fireman?' Angela asked Frank.

Amanda remembered that the reason Frank and Bridie lived with the Hallorans was because Frank was out of work. But rather than anyone being embarrassed by the blunt question, he answered quickly, "Neither my father nor my uncle is a fireman. That's how it works."

"That doesn't sound fair," Angela persisted.

He shrugged.

The bowls had made their way around the table and then Mr. Halloran asked for preferences as each person handed him their plates.

"Oh, the gravy," Mrs. Halloran said, getting up quickly. "Can't have a family meal without forgetting something," she muttered.

"Good gravy!" Sean said.

This was not like the quiet meals that Amanda was used to at home where one of the maids dished out the servings and left the family to sedate comments about the food, the weather, or the state of the world. And sometimes a bit of teasing between the sisters. Here several conversations were going on at once to the accompaniment of silverware clattering on dishes, Sean's teasing his younger sister, Imogen's banging on the highchair tray and then Mrs. Halloran's attempting to be heard above the noise.

"How did you two meet?" she asked, looking at both of them as if allowing for them to get their stories straight.

"There was an incident at the Valentine Ball last year while I was on duty. Amanda was there for her sister's coming-out."

"Coming out of where?" Angela asked, and everyone laughed.

"When a young girl is a debutante, they say she is coming out," Brendan explained.

"Coming out to the notice of society," Amanda added. "Meaning she can date and go to parties without a chaperone."

Angela looked at her father as if to verify that such strange things existed in the world. "Chaperone?"

"And no, you won't be having a coming-out party," Bridie said.

"Your confirmation hoolie was enough for our family," Mr. Halloran chuckled.

"Holy and hoolie," Sean said.

"It might have been my party, but it was all your friends. I had to memorize the whole catechism, wear that silly robe and beanie, and then have the bishop slap me for my efforts."

Patrick laughed. "He's got a good right hook, I hear."

"Oh, don't exaggerate," Mrs. Halloran said. "The both of you." She shook her head.

"How's your new place?" Patrick asked Brendan.

"Very quiet."

Everyone laughed and Sean practically shouted, "I can't hear you."

The banter continued and at least one conversation was about the state of the economy, another about what local businesses has closed and what had opened in their place, a third describing new neighbors moving in down the street, the death of another neighbor peppered with updates on other family members. Amanda was overwhelmed by the rapidity of the speech and the changing currents in conversation and paid attention to her meal. All too soon it came to an end with the conversation dying down.

"Well, who's for dessert?" Mrs. Halloran asked.

"You mean who are we eating for dessert?" Sean asked.

"You need to write a joke book," Brendan said.

"That's a great idea," he answered.

"Ahem. I was just *joking*."

"What are we going to have?" Mr. Halloran asked.

Bridie, Angela and Mrs. Halloran got up and collected the plates and Amanda looked at Brendan, wondering if she was supposed to assist as well. He shook his head. "You're the guest," he said quietly, but his brother overheard him.

"The guest gets to wash the pots," Sean said, laughing at his remark and getting a glare from his father.

"Save it for your joke book."

"We have ice cream from that new place that opened up," Mrs. Halloran said, going through the swinging door to the kitchen. The sound of plates being scraped came from the other room, the water ran in the sink and then silence as the dessert was being prepared. Angela came back in and collected the remaining plates, took them into the kitchen and some minutes later Mrs. Halloran returned with a tray with bowls of vanilla ice cream topped with fudge sauce, followed by her two daughters carrying the same.

"Oh, my favorite!" Sean said.

"Mama makes the fudge sauce from scratch," Angela said as they passed the bowls out.

"This is wonderful, Mrs. Halloran. As was the rest of the meal," Amanda said.

"Does your mother have any special recipes?" Angela asked.

Amanda paused. "She doesn't cook much but she loves scones."

"I haven't had those since I was in Ireland," Patrick said. "The butter there is out of this world. The milk and cream are so rich."

"When were you there?" Amanda asked.

"Two years ago, on a recruiting trip for the seminary. A beautiful place but the poverty is terrible. So many bright young men with not much of a future. There was a sponsor from Boston who sent a few of us there to scout for likely candidates for the priesthood."

"Many are called but few are chosen," Mr. Halloran said. "My parents and those of the Missus came over—had to leave—and we're glad they did. It was hard times for everyone then."

"And doesn't seem to have got much better," Patrick said.

"Oh, forgot to put the coffee on," Mrs. Halloran said, popping up to do so. A telephone rang in the kitchen, and they could hear her answering. She opened the swinging door to the dining room and said, "Bren, it's for you." She held out the receiver as he stepped into the kitchen.

"Dominick—what's going on?"

"I tried you at your apartment and then, on a whim, remembered your parents' number. A cleaning lady in City Hall found someone in the basement. He's dead. Can you come around?"

"Sure, sure. I'll be there directly." He hung up the phone. To his mother's inquiring look he said, "Work."

"On a Sunday? Surely not."

"Evil never rests," he said, returning to the dining room. "Sorry, I've got to go. Work beckons." There was a wail from the younger folks.

"I'll finish your ice cream," Sean volunteered.

Amanda looked up. What was she supposed to do? Sit here until he got done?

"Why don't you come with me?" Brendan said. "I can drop you off at home."

She expressed her thanks to his parents for the meal and their kind attentions as Brendan hustled her into her coat and out the door.

"Don't you dare drop me off at home. I'm coming with you," she said.

Chapter 6

"Are you just going to sit in the car while I go into City Hall?" he asked as he started the car.

"Of course not. I'm going in with you."

"I don't think that's a good idea," he said.

"Nonsense. You know I always hear or see something that you folks overlook."

He glanced over at her as he put the car into gear. "You may come with me, but you are not part of this investigation."

She didn't respond.

"Dominick didn't give me any details anyway."

"We'll see," she said primly. After a pause she added, "I am so impressed with your mother. Cooking a meal for your big family! Three times a day!"

"Not unlike most of the world," Brendan said.

"I do know how to cook," she said defensively.

"I wasn't aware that you could. Not that I don't doubt you would do a smashing job of it."

She shot him a look out of the corner of her eye.

"What's your favorite thing to make," he asked.

She thought for a minute. "Welsh rarebit."

"Welsh rabbit—what's that?"

"It's like fondue."

"I've never had fondue either."

"Welsh rarebit is melted cheese on toasted bread. Fondue is melted cheese that you dip pieces of bread into."

"That's a meal?"

"Of course not. You have a side salad of some kind and… it's very French. Or maybe Swiss, I can't remember."

"I'll be happy to sample either one sometime if you make it."

Amanda thought of the logistics of such a proposition. She couldn't invite him to her house for dinner and then pop into the kitchen to make the meal. Cook wouldn't stand for it, and it would be downright strange. She knew he had his own apartment, but she could hardly set up shop there to make a meal. What would people think?

Noticing her furrowed brow he added, "But if it's too complicated to arrange, let's continue to sample the bounty of Boston's fine cuisine. We've been stuck on Catalano's, which is an excellent place to be stuck, but there are wonderful oyster bars, seafood restaurants, German places and old-fashioned chop houses."

She instantly thought of the place that Doctor Fred Browne, her former boyfriend, had taken her to cement his proposal of marriage that she had politely declined. She wondered if part of the reason for her response was being in that staid place, imagining that her life as wife to a doctor would be just as predictable and unexciting.

Brendan pulled up in front of City Hall where an ambulance and Dominick's car were parked. They climbed the steps and tried the doors, which were locked until a security guard got up from a desk in the lobby and waddled to the door.

"Detective Halloran," Brendan said, showing his badge and ushering Amanda in before him. "Where is everyone?"

"In the basement."

He had no idea how to access the basement until the guard pointed to a door at the end of the hall.

"Thanks." Opening the door and descending the stairs, he was surprised to see that it wasn't some dark, dank storage area but an active office space with a sign and an arrow indicating, "Inspections."

"What do they inspect?" Amanda asked.

"Things like ongoing construction, boilers, property issues, vacant buildings. I know they go out if there's been a fire to determine if the dwelling is livable after the firemen have left. I'm sure you've seen those 'Caution' or 'Danger, do not enter' signs."

She couldn't recall ever seeing any such thing in Beacon Hill, just wooden sawhorses blocking off a hole in the street when someone was digging. Dominick was at the bottom of the stairs waiting for them.

"What took you so long?"

"You well know. You called me at my parents' home. Sunday dinner."

"He's back here," Dominick said after a nod toward Amanda. She followed them, and he looked at her askance as if to inquire what she was doing there. She didn't notice; she was busy taking in the warren of desks and bulletin boards in the bullpen area and the vast array of pipes strung across the ceiling.

They made their way toward the back of the room where the ambulance men were waiting before moving the body. Off to the side was a middle-aged woman who held a damp rag in her hand as if not knowing where to put it. Sprawled on the floor partly under one of the desks was a body in a gray uniform shirt and dark pants.

"Inspector?" Halloran asked Dominick.

"Looks like it. We didn't want to move him until you got here. The Medical Examiner is off fishing somewhere today, but we can't just leave this guy here."

"Hit on the back of the head?" Halloran said, judging from the blood in his hair. "Let's turn him carefully," he added, and they did so, revealing a nametag on his chest, Kehoe. There was a cut on his face and some bruising. "Whether he was in a fight or got the damage when he fell, we might never know." He looked at the man's hands and saw scraped knuckles.

"Fought back before he bought it perhaps," Dominick said.

"I suppose you can take him now," Halloran said to the two attendants.

Seeing the woman standing there very still, he asked her if she was the one who discovered the man.

"I came to clean today because my daughter was sick yesterday. I usually come on Saturday."

"Did you hear anything or see anything suspicious?"

"No. The other woman starts on the top floor and works her way down. I start on the first floor and work my way down. Empty the trash, sweep the floor. They don't let me touch the papers on the desks or anything."

"So, you've been here since the morning?"

"About eleven o'clock."

"I'm surprised the security guard didn't find him first," Amanda said.

"He doesn't walk around like a watchman. He just sits at the desk in the lobby and lets anyone in who is working on the weekend."

"Even if he had put his head in the room and looked around, he wouldn't have seen him," Dominick commented.

"Are there many people who come in on the weekend?" Halloran's experience with civil service workers were that they were strictly nine-to-five people, even though he knew the Mayor often stopped in on weekends.

"I don't know. I'm busy working. Ask the guard. But I've never seen anyone before when I was down here," she said.

The attendants had brought in a stretcher from the ambulance earlier; now they carefully lifted the body onto it and covered it with a sheet. Hoisting it up between them, they went out of the room.

"Can I go now?" the woman asked.

"Can I ask you a few more questions?" Without waiting for an answer, he went on. "Do you start at the front of the room and work your way back? Or the other way around?"

She looked puzzled at what she considered a stupid question. "I start at the first trash can I come to."

"So, by the time you got to the back of the room, you had already dumped most of the cans?" He gestured to the large receptacle on wheels nearby that was more than half full.

"Yes."

"Do we have your name and contact information?" Halloran asked.

"He took it already," she said, pointing to Dominick.

"Thank you. You can go now."

She slung the rag over the side of the receptacle and began to wheel it toward the door.

"Wait. Please leave that here," Halloran said.

She stared at him. "Fine by me. I'm done anyway."

When it was just the three of them, Halloran said, "There might be something interesting in that big can."

Dominick shot him a look as if wondering if he was going to be the one to sift through the garbage.

"I agree," Amanda said.

The two men looked at her.

"Why, did you want to help?" Dominick asked, looking at her white gloves.

"What I meant was, if she started at the front of the room and then stopped when she discovered the body, she certainly wouldn't have emptied his ashtray and trash can before going up to tell the security guard that she had found a body. But his trash and the ashtray have been emptied."

"Exactly," Halloran said. "I don't know where they keep their cleaning equipment in the building—probably in some storage closet. There's a chance someone dumped this guy's trash in the big can knowing that another pile would land on top of it."

"You think there was something important in the trash?" Amanda asked but got no answer.

"If she starts upstairs and works her way down to the basement, there's more trash in there than the stuff from here," Dominick said.

"And why would someone dump the ashtray, too? Maybe either the victim or the killer or both were smokers?" Amanda asked.

Halloran gave her a look.

"I'm just trying to help," she said.

"Let's get this can back to the office and have someone look through it carefully."

"I'll get the recruits to do it," Dominick suggested.

"Naturally, we're not going to dig around in there. I don't suppose there are any old banana peels, rotten eggs or rats in it anyway."

Amanda gave an involuntary shudder.

"Let's take a look around at the rest of this place," Halloran suggested.

The desks were arranged symmetrically in neat rows and by tacit agreement, the two detectives each took one side of the room and, moving slowly, looked for anything suspicious on top of the desks and opened the drawers to find citation booklets, some files, pencils and other sorts of paperwork. No bloody weapon. No other bodies.

When they were done, Dominick pushed the can toward the door but, before they left, Halloran took a handkerchief out of his pocket, picked up the ashtray and, looking around, found a manila envelope that he could put it in.

"Our guy might have been clever enough to dump the papers and whatever else he was trying to cover up, but we might be able to find fingerprints on this. I'll drop you back at your house and you can tell your parents all about your eventful meal with the Halloran tribe. And kindly leave out this footnote. They've got enough on their mind with Louisa's antics."

Chapter 7

The two detectives went to the morgue on Monday morning after their staff meeting to look at the body of Inspector Kehoe and see if the Medical Examiner had any preliminary information for them.

"Catch anything?" Dominick asked. "Kind of early in the season."

"Sometimes it's just great to be out there. But it's getting to be the end of cod season. Not my favorite fish, but the wife likes it that I get it fresh for her. And it's our heritage, after all," he added with a smile that wrinkled his sunburnt face. "Aren't we the land of the bean and the cod?" Changing topics, he added, "I had a gander at your guy in there." He walked in front of them and grabbed a white coat off the rack just inside the double doors.

"Looks like he was in a rough-and-tumble with someone and likely not his first." He carefully buttoned the lab coat up and readjusted his glasses before the pulling the sheet back from the man's face.

Dominick grunted at the bruises on the man's face.

"Those might be from a blow, or perhaps he fell on his face. Is that how he landed? Did you happen to notice?"

"We found him face down, which doesn't mean that's how he originally lay," Halloran said.

"What felled him was a significant blow to the back of the head. With a ball peen hammer, no less. Nicely rounded wound expertly landed. Probably fractured his skull, but we'll see later today."

Dominick winced.

"Look at his hands," Doctor Lindforth said. "Working man, but you knew that already. Grease under the nails, well-muscled arms and look at the scars on the knuckles under the fresh abrasions. Maybe a former Golden Gloves guy, a pugnacious person or someone who was uncommonly clumsy. Broke his nose sometime back, too. I'll go with the hot temper theory."

"We'll be talking to his supervisor and fellow inspectors today and I suppose we'll find out more about what this Mr. Kehoe was like. And what the heck he was doing in his workplace on a Sunday," Halloran said, turning to go.

"You may have found him on Sunday, but it didn't happen then. It looks as if he died a full day before," Lindforth said. "I'll get back to you with a more precise window of time."

"DO those inspectors even work on the weekends? I mean, if they're called out after a house fire to determine if the structure is habitable, it stands to reason someone must be on call," Dominick said.

"Good point. But if City Hall is closed on the weekends, the security guard must have been familiar with who had access to the building. And if the inspector was on call, is there a direct line to the inspectors' area? Was there a switchboard operator also on duty? How would he know to respond to an incident?"

"Is there another way into the basement area?"

"Probably. I can't imagine the Mayor condoning some scruffy, blue-collar guys rubbing shoulders with the folks that go upstairs."

"Let's go to City Hall and see how this guy's co-workers are reacting."

At the beginning of the workweek, there was not a chance of pulling up to the building and parking out front as they had the day before. They circled the block twice before even seeing a 'No Parking' sign for a space where they could pull in and put their police card on the inside of the windshield. A cold wind still blew up from the harbor even though it was early April. Easter coming in two weeks' time made everyone think it was spring, but one last freak snowstorm might come before things warmed up for good.

The security guard behind the desk in the lobby was not the same one as the day before. Still, this man might give them some of the information they sought. They introduced themselves, showing their badges, and asked for his name and how long he had worked there.

As expected, he looked appropriately intimidated.

"I've done this for about four years," he said. "Nothing like this has ever happened before."

"So, you know what happened?"

"Sure, they told me first thing when I got here. Come to think of it, another man died once upstairs, but that was a heart attack that couldn't be helped. Not attacked, like this one."

"Who said he was attacked?" Dominick asked.

Flustered, the guard answered, "It's what everyone is saying, that's all."

"Hmm," Dominick muttered and took a small notepad from his coat pocket and a pencil and began to write.

"Who has access to the building on the weekends?"

"I worked Saturday, not Sunday."

"That's not what I asked."

"The doors are locked and that's why there is a guard on duty to let people in."

"Anybody who comes to the door?"

"No. The routine is that after hours, we have a roster of all the employees, and they have to identify themselves."

"How do they do that?"

The guard raised his light eyebrows and thought a moment. "They tell us who they are, we check the roster and then we can let them in. We write time in and the time out, too."

"Do you ask them to show identification of any kind?"

"No. We know them by sight. At least I do."

"Have you ever had anyone try to gain entry after hours who you didn't recognize?"

"Absolutely not. Well, once someone knocked on the glass doors to ask directions, but that's all."

"And how late do you stay?"

"If I'm working the late shift, I clock out at midnight. There's an alarm that we set before we go. So, it's important that we make sure anyone who has come into the building is gone before we set it."

"Are there usually people working that late?" Dominick asked.

"Sometimes the Mayor has a late meeting. But not often."

"Is there other access to the basement that you know of?"

"Sure. The inspectors come and go all day long, so they park out in back and come in the basement door."

"Is that wired to the alarm system?"

He thought a moment. "I don't know. I expect so. Maybe you should talk to Mr. Bremer."

"Who's he?"

"He's the supervisor of the inspection group."

"Do you know if he's in?"

"I'm not sure. During a regular workday, I don't check people in. And he wouldn't come through the front anyhow."

"I guess we'd better have a talk with Mr. Bremer," Halloran said, and thanked the guard for his time. "Let's take the elevator," he suggested to Dominick.

The basement was cool and quiet, and they saw the door to the inspectors' area was open to the hall and walked into what seemed to be an impromptu staff meeting.

Mr. Bremer, the only one standing, noticed the visitors and stopped mid-sentence. "Can I help you?"

"Detectives Halloran and Barone. Sorry to interrupt, but we need to talk to you."

All heads swiveled in their direction.

"All right. Everyone stays here until I'm done." He led the detectives to an office along the wall that at least had some light coming in from a clerestory window that gave view to the feet and ankles of passersby on the street above. He closed the door, gestured to two chairs, now empty of papers, that faced his battleship grey metal desk and sat behind it. His pale face and paunchy stomach labeled him a lifelong bureaucrat.

He looked them over and said, "I've seen a lot in my time here at the City, but this is a nasty business."

"We need to get some background on Mr. Kehoe and how things work here."

"Such as?"

"The man was killed here, which suggests some ongoing animosity. There was also probably a fight before the lethal blow. Do you have any thoughts about that?"

"I don't like to speak ill of the dead, but Kehoe was not the most stellar of employees. I just chewed him out on Friday after a member of the public complained about him."

Halloran waited and realized he was going to have to prompt the man every step of the way. "About what?"

"These men have a broad scope of work to do. We don't issue the permits for work; we do the back end of making sure the work was done correctly. One group inspects boilers and other mechanical work, another building permit compliance and another exterior property issues. Kehoe was part of the last group."

"He was probably out and about most of the day, then?"

"Of course. All the men are. In all kinds of weather."

"What was the complaint about him?"

"It wasn't the first time. There's this woman who has appointed herself a watchdog on City activities. You know, calling the Police Chief if she thinks there are bad people creeping around her neighborhood. That kind of thing. But also calling us about her neighbors' infractions and violations. I guess one of them got fed up with her ratting everyone else out and called one in on her. So, Kehoe goes out to the house and talks to the man of the house on Thursday, not knowing that his mother-in-law is this Mrs. Costello. Kehoe not only tells the guy that he must fix the sidewalk—which is on public property—he suggests that he knows someone who can do it for him. He's got a pocketful of cards of his pals who do repair work, and you can bet that he gets a kickback on it."

"Interesting racket," Dominick said.

"I heard he might be doing something like that before, but this time he was caught at it. Pled innocent. Of course."

"Do you think someone would kill him for it?"

Mr. Bremer closed his eyes and shrugged. "Who knows what else he was up to? These guys take an oath when they're sworn in as City employees, but the reality is they are out and about by themselves all day. No telling what they may get up to." Sensing an objection from the detectives, he continued. "Now don't go suggesting we send them out in pairs. That's ridiculous. That puts our manpower at fifty per cent. It's how the system has always worked, and we just deal with the bad apples as best we can."

"What happened to the files or cases he was working on?"

"I've divvied them up already."

"Those papers may contain something that would help us narrow down who did this."

Bremer gave a snort. "Not likely. He was a master at having the thinnest work files I've ever seen."

"We were curious about security and were told there is an entrance to the outside from the basement."

"Sure. You want to see it?" He got up and led them back out through the bullpen where the men were milling around, some talking, some smoking, waiting for the resumption of their meeting. Bremer preceded the detectives down the corridor in one direction and pointed to a door that opened with a steel push bar. He opened it to an area with large garbage bins and stairs to the street. Closing it, he walked to the other end of the corridor where there was a similar door, this one propped open with a brick.

"What the...?" he sputtered, pushing the door fully open onto a parking lot where two inspectors leaned against a truck, smoking. They snapped to attention and crushed out the cigarettes.

"Sorry, boss," one said as they slid past back into the building.

"Is that a regular thing?" Halloran asked.

"Stepping out for a smoke?" Bremer asked.

"No. Propping the door."

He scowled and, kicking the brick aside, said, "Unfortunately, yes. I guess it's too much trouble to find the keys in your pocket and unlock the door to get back in." He let the door slam behind him. The detectives looked at each other.

"Tell me, are any of your staff on call for emergencies?"

"No. They should be, but that budget got cut long ago, much to the annoyance of the men. It was a way to make extra money, something everybody's in need of these days. If there's a fire or other emergency, we let the fire department or health department take the lead. We've let them make the call on whether a building ought to be condemned or at least not allow any entry. It's a clumsy system, but what are you going to do?"

"Can you think of any reason Inspector Kehoe would be here on a Saturday?"

"I thought you found him on a Sunday?" Bremer asked.

"That's when we found him, but he died the day or night before."

Bremer rubbed his chin. "No reason on earth he should have been here. Believe me, he was the last person to want to put in extra hours without getting paid."

"So, you don't have your men on call after hours or on the weekends?"

"Can't afford to. Everybody's budget got cut after the crash. No more time and a half and overtime for these guys."

"That could be an incentive to look for additional income streams," Dominick observed,

"Aside from a possibly irate citizen, can you think of anyone who might have animosity toward Kehoe?" Halloran asked. "One of his fellow employees?"

Bremer scoffed. "I've got a roomful of guys who thought he was a goof-off, a clown who didn't pull his weight. And there's an ex-wife somewhere. I hope you've got enough pages in that notebook."

"I can see you're busy this morning, but let your folks know that we'll need to talk to them sometime soon," Halloran said, heading toward the elevators.

Once they were out of earshot, he added, "Notice how he side-stepped every question?"

"Your tax dollars at work," Dominick muttered.

Chapter 8

Mr. Bremer slammed the door from the corridor to the bullpen as viciously as he could and glared at the men whose full attention he now had. "Well, gentlemen," he said in a patently false tone. "I think you could get out of your chairs and stand up properly for this tongue-lashing." He waited while they got up, Slater leaning against one of the desks looking bored. Bremer stared at him, and he straightened up, wiping all expression from his face.

"So much to share with you. You all know Kehoe was killed. Right here in this room. Right there, as a matter of fact." He pointed to the empty desk and those standing nearest stepped away. "You all knew him. A wise guy. We got reports about him out in the field, and they weren't compliments, either. He came as close to shaking people down as possible, except one lady was on to his shenanigans and called me about it. That tells me that it probably wasn't the first time. And since you fellows are such good colleagues, my guess is that you knew he did it, and some of you might have thought, '*Why not give it a try?*'" He stopped and licked his lips before continuing in the same, even tone. "And I'll tell you why you won't give it a try. Because if I even get a whiff that you're doing something like that, I'll fire you in a second." He snapped his finger, then stopped and let the words sink in.

"Now, the fine detectives have told me that it looks like Kehoe was in a fight with his attacker. Certainly not the little old lady who called in a complaint on him—why would she? She had already inflicted the damage on him. But I know some of you have had words with him in the past so I'm giving you the opportunity now to let me know if you were in here over the weekend when he was here."

The room was silent, with every man looking directly at the boss.

"That's good. But just to be sure, I'd like to check your hands and arms to look for bruises or signs of a fight."

"Come on, Mr. Bremer, a lot of us do heavy work in this job and back at our homes on the weekend," one inspector said.

"I box at the gym on Saturday," another said.

There was an undercurrent of muttering.

"Inspector Torgan if you don't mind? I know you and he had words on Friday."

Torgan's eyes widened, and he was stock still.

"Come on, show me your hands and roll up your sleeves."

The man hesitated and said, "I was doing stonework at my church on Saturday and my hands are a mess."

"Let's take a look," the boss said.

Torgan's face became red, and he blurted, "No. And I have to talk to you in your office."

The others were astounded at his bold statement. They knew him for an odd duck, keeping to himself and always spouting about the Bible. But fist fighting with Kehoe? That seemed unlikely. They looked at one another and the boss led Torgan into his office and closed the door, thinking he had solved the mystery already. They stood facing each other.

"Do you have something to tell me?" Bremer asked.

"Yes." He bit his lip. "It's true about working at my church and scraping my knuckles, but I don't want to show my arms in public."

"Why?"

"This may not be important to you, but the Bible has strict commands about defiling your body." He paused while his boss wondered where this was going. "I haven't always lived in a God-fearing way. I led a terrible life of sin and rowdy behavior when I worked on the docks. Like many there, I got some tattoos." He positioned himself to make sure that nobody out in the bullpen could see through the glass in the boss's door what he was about to reveal to him. He slowly rolled up the left sleeve of his uniform to uncover a mermaid on his forearm, flowers and hearts on his biceps and a woman's name, which his boss assumed did not belong to the man's current wife.

"I don't want anybody to see these. I never uncover my arms. Not even at home. And I don't want some of these godless men to see and mock me for being a hypocrite. Because I am not. I have given myself over to the Lord entirely. These tattoos represent my sinful past and if I could erase them I would. But I can't. And I don't want to show them to anyone else. You have been the exception today." He rolled the sleeve down.

Mr. Bremer sighed. "I understand your point of view. I can't see if you've got bruises underneath all that ink anyhow."

"With all my heart and soul, I tried to like Inspector Kehoe, but I confess that I did not. He had no morality that I could see and laughed at mine."

They stood looking at one another. Then Mr. Bremer opened the door and they both walked out.

After a pause he said, "Well, it isn't my job to find out if one of you had a fight with Kehoe and killed him," the boss said to the group. "That's up to the police. They'll do their job and God help you if it is one of you. I'm sorry to say, you'll probably be looking over your shoulders from now on, not knowing who to trust here, much less who out there in our fair city has a grudge and might not be satisfied that it has been resolved. Think about that when you're sitting at your desk, writing up your notes from the field and feel the presence of someone standing behind you. Think about that when you have to confront an irate citizen about a complaint from a neighbor. Think about that when you have to do a boiler inspection and go down to the cellar with someone. Just the two of you. Alone in a dark basement. Have a good week out there, gentlemen."

Before the elevator doors had closed on the two detectives, they heard Mr. Bremer slam the door. They waited until they were in motion before speaking.

"I don't like the setup here at all," Dominick said. "Two doors to the outside and one of them propped open."

"If they all have keys to the building, any one of them could have had access at whatever point during the weekend the murder occurred. And if anyone saw one of them entering City Hall that way, it was business as usual," Halloran said. "It's hard to imagine that some member of the public was able to gain access."

"Unless he was followed in by someone."

"Or if he lured them back to the office to accept a payoff and give the person the paperwork cancelling the citation."

"Someone could just as easily come from an upstairs office down to the basement without being seen," Dominick said.

"That occurred to me. But in that case, the security guard would have had to check them in. Let's get the roster from Saturday and Sunday."

They stopped at the guard's desk and asked to look at the weekend's visitors to the building. They recognized the Mayor's name, of course, and that of Henry Rogers, his aide, and a woman's name.

"Who's that?"

"The Mayor's secretary."

"And these people?"

"They work in the finance and budget department. They come in on weekends sometimes. That person had left his briefcase in the office, he said, and went to get it."

"How do you know that?" Halloran asked.

"Because I was on duty Saturday. He wasn't gone very long by the looks of it."

"And what about the Sunday roster?"

He turned to the previous page, glanced at it and showed it to them.

"Looks like nobody came in. Not unusual."

They thanked him and Halloran said to Dominick as they went out the front door, "The Medical Examiner didn't clarify when he died on Saturday. I want to know if he can get more specific as to the time." He rolled his eyes in frustration. "Let's get back to the office," he said. "If I can remember where I parked the car." He stopped short as he saw Amanda coming up the steps.

"Hello!" she said brightly. "You're here again."

"I fear we're going to be here quite a lot. Many people to interview. What are you doing here?"

"I have a meeting with the Mayor about clinic staffing. He may have found a solution to the problem of not having an assigned receptionist for the North End clinic. We can't keep using Mr. Barlow's secretary, Miss Bailey. Not that she doesn't do a good job, but it takes her away from her work for him two days a week and that's likely to make him cranky about the clinic expansion."

"When you're done with your meeting, let's have lunch," Halloran said.

"That sounds wonderful. Where shall I meet you?"

"Oh, you know. Catalano's, of course."

They smiled at each other, and Dominick felt distinctly like a third wheel.

"You'll join us, won't you?" Amanda asked.

"I've got a previous engagement," he lied.

Chapter 9

Brendan Halloran was already seated when Amanda came into the restaurant to the rapturous reception of Mr. Catalano, whose daughter, Simona, now worked for the Burnsides.

"How happy we are to see you," he said, clasping his hands together in front of his chest.

"How could we take lunch anywhere else?" she asked as Brendan stood up and pulled out a chair for her.

"If it weren't Prohibition, I would pour you each a glass of wine," the proprietor said.

"It doesn't seem to bother anybody else," Brendan murmured under his breath. He looked at Amanda, her cheeks rosy from the chilly air and thought her the most beautiful woman he knew. She smiled back at him, which made his heart clench.

"Good meeting with the Mayor?" he asked.

"I should say so. He is intent on making his mark on this city. With his connections, he managed to get Catholic Social Services to round up volunteers to act as receptionists not just for the North End, but also for the original Mercy Hospital clinic."

"Impressive, indeed."

"They are volunteers and, of course, they have found several women who speak Italian, so that is one problem solved." She took a sip of water. "How is your case going?"

He exhaled. "The man who was killed was evidently not well liked by his peers according to his boss. So, not only was he up to no good in the wide world, but the home team was not in his court, either."

"Oh, dear. What kind of 'no good' was he up to?"

"THESE INSPECTORS ARE OUT and about on their own —mostly because they can't afford to send them out in pairs—and that, of course, opens up opportunities for malfeasance."

She tilted her head to one side as if to query what that meant.

"There are ways that people in that position can suggest or imply that greasing the palm could make problems go away."

"Does that happen often?" she asked, never having been in a position to have witnessed that.

He shrugged. "Who knows? But the opportunity is there, in any case."

"If others were doing it, why would they be upset with him? Because it could draw attention to them?"

"That's possible. Or maybe they didn't have the nerve to try. It seems he was not one to stick his hand out for cash but had a more sophisticated method where he would tell the offender that he knew of someone who could do the work to alleviate the violation. And, of course, the people he recommended were friends or colleagues of his who would give him a kickback for the recommendation."

"That might be hard to prove if so many people participated in it," she said.

"Or maybe easy because one of them might cave into police pressure and blow the top off the entire scheme. In any case, it was a clever way to handle those situations. Unfortunately for the inspector, the actual owner of one house was someone familiar with the ways of the street, and she called his boss almost immediately, accusing the inspector of trying to bilk the family. And the next day, the Mayor excoriated the department directors about dishonesty and they, in turn, did the same for their staff all the way down the line. Everybody in City government had got the message on Friday and then this man is killed over the weekend."

"Wait, you said over the weekend? I thought he was killed on Sunday?"

"The Medical Examiner says it was Saturday."

"And no one saw anything?" Amanda asked. Sensing someone at her shoulder she gave a bit of a gasp, but it only Mr. Catalano seeking to take their order. She gave a laugh. "I was very involved in your comments, Brendan."

"What do you have today?" he asked the owner.

"Chicken Fiorentina and Lasagna Bolognese. There is Italian wedding soup, too."

They both sighed at the difficulty of the choice.

"How about we get both and we can share?" Brendan suggested.

This was new approach to dining for Amanda although it made perfect sense. "Yes, let's."

"And a cup of soup for me," Brendan said.

"I'll bring the bread," Mr. Catalano said.

When he was out of earshot, Amanda asked, "What did you find out about the ashtray?"

"I saw the tech puff dust on it this morning and the preliminary judgment was that it was covered in many smudged fingerprints. He was going to go over it more carefully today to see if he could lift any clean ones off."

"I don't suppose anyone actually cleaned the ashtrays at any time in the past year," she commented.

"Based on what the place looked like, you are probably correct. But we may get lucky."

Brendan paused a moment. "I don't want to sound harsh, but I'm only sharing basic information because you were there with me when we first encountered the body. I can't say anything more as it could compromise the case."

She widened her eyes. "I don't see how it could be compromised. My family has no interest in this kind of thing and I'm not going to let them know of it or it will throw them into a tizzy. It's not as if I know any of the inspection staff.

The only folks I know in City Hall are the Mayor, Henry and Nora and I won't be talking to them about this. But your work is so interesting, I can't help inquiring." She paused. "Do they ever hire female detectives?"

"You're not getting any ideas in that direction, I hope." Brendan deftly changed the topic.

"What's your impression of the Mayor?"

"He has the uncanny ability of knowing what you're going to say next."

"What do you mean?"

"Of course, he knows of my connection with the hospital, but he didn't know that I was going to ask for his help in getting assistance with staffing. Yet he was the one who brought up the idea of using the Catholic Charities volunteers."

"That's because he is a good politician who can see one step ahead of everyone else. I wouldn't play chess with him. And he also has an able aide in Henry, who keeps his eyes and ears open."

"Still. It was rather unnerving."

Mr. Catalano brought bread in a basket and the cup of soup and said the food would be ready soon.

"Another thing. The Mayor said to say hello to you."

Brendan stopped short while reaching for the basket. "What?"

"He did. I played it very cool and made it seem as if I were puzzled at best. Does he suspect we know one another? Does he have spies everywhere?"

"Have I ever called you on my work telephone to ask you out?" he asked.

"No. Only in person."

"Then it didn't come from listening in on our conversations."

"What do you mean?"

"You know you must go through a switchboard to get my department. There's a possibility that an operator is listening in."

Mr. Catalano arrived with the main dishes, delicious aromas wafting in the air. "Who gets the chicken?" he asked.

"I suppose I'll start with that." She looked down at the flattened cutlet of chicken breast nestled in spinach napped with cream sauce. "On second thought, I don't know that I want to share this," she said, looking over at his lasagna.

"Don't you think there is something special about sharing a meal?" he asked. "I mean, actually sharing a meal?"

She took a deep breath. "Look who's getting ideas now?"

Chapter 10

Halloran and Dominick faced the daunting task of interviewing all the inspectors, which they thought might take days, until they considered using a few of the recruits to assist. The young men would consider it a pat on the back after having sifted through the trash from the basement of City Hall.

O'Rourke, who was the self-appointed leader of the group of three recruits, presented the findings of the trash pile to the two detectives in a methodical way as he stood at attention in front of them.

"Sir, we have sorted through the evidence, and we can report the following. The material falls into several categories: some food refuse, smoking detritus and paper litter, and we have separated these accordingly. I would recommend that the food refuse be relegated permanently to the trash bin. Likewise, the cigarette and cigar butts. The paper might prove the most informative."

"What did you find?"

"There were memos from other departments, copies of citation forms that were partially filled out and then crumpled up and discarded, scraps of paper with telephone numbers on them and pink telephone messages that an operator must have taken down and sent to the department."

"Let's see the paper pile," Halloran said, motioning to O'Rourke to lead him to where they had done their work, a small room down the end of the hall.

The pile represented the remains of the workweek of twelve inspectors, all of whom seemed to use preprinted citation slips that separated the original from the office copy with a thin sheet of carbon paper. The men wrote the citation out by hand in pencil, fountain pen being too messy in the field, and gave the original to the property owner or homeowner and the office copy to somebody to log in. They were surprised to see several originals along with the copy rolled in a ball and discarded.

"What do you make of this?" Halloran asked Dominick.

"Someone made a mistake?"

"Someone changed their mind?" Halloran suggested. "None of these are signed, but I wonder if we can track the number printed on the top to a particular inspector. We can ask when we do our interviews. Good work, O'Rourke. I'm going to start with another visit to the basement workplace to get a better idea of how Bremer makes the assignments, dig deeper on the nature of a typical workday and set up a schedule for the interviews with his men. Dominick, why don't you see if you can use your considerable charm to find out if the person who complained about the inspector called the Mayor's office first?"

"Someone said the Mayor was referring to the police department in his tirade, not the inspection group."

"Since I wasn't there, I don't know, but that's how the Chief interpreted it. Maybe there was more than one complaint lodged in a short time and that tipped the scales for the Mayor."

"I'll see what I can do," Dominick shrugged, not convinced he could get that level of information out of anyone.

Halloran didn't bother to call Mr. Bremer before showing up at the door to the subterranean bullpen where he found him alone in his office. Knocking on the open door, Halloran smiled at the startled man and asked if he could ask a few questions.

Bremer got up abruptly and said, "Of course. Let me just close the door. I don't know if anybody is out there, but no one needs to overhear our conversation."

Halloran sat down in one of the chairs facing the desk and put his hat on the other while taking a notebook out of his pocket. "It would be helpful to understand how this place works in greater detail," he said, making a vague gesture with his hand.

"What do you mean?" Bremer folded his hands on the desktop, appearing to be relaxed, but Halloran could see the knuckles were taut.

"I understand that certain men do specific kinds of inspections, like the boilers or confirming building permits, but what about if a member of the public contacts you? And a better question is: do members of the public contact you?"

Bremer laughed. "Oh, yes. You can bet they do. But let me get back to how the whole thing was set up. I didn't create this department; I inherited it. It's not a perfect system but we make it work. Boilers need inspection during installation and then they are on a calendar re-inspection basis. That's what those inspectors do, and they are kept busy, let me tell you. We don't issue permits for construction, plumbing or electrical—that's the Building Department. But when the work is completed and the architect, builder or homeowner needs a certificate of occupancy, we've got four guys who are assigned to make sure the work was done correctly."

"That's odd. Why don't the people who issue the permits follow up when the work is finished?" Halloran asked.

"That would be too simple, my friend." He laughed again, leaning back in his chair. "The reason is those folks upstairs who issue the permits have an education. That's why they are not stuck in the basement. They're high school graduates, some of them even college graduates and their Director has an architecture degree. White collar boys, every one of them. They don't get their hands dirty going out in the field, wiggling through crawl spaces to see if the pipes are connected to the sewer."

"That's a reasonable explanation," Halloran conceded. "But there might be some difference in interpretation between what was planned and how it was executed."

"It can happen. But we don't usually have many complaints about that."

"What do people call you about?"

"Some people in this city are always looking for a fight. Neighbor against neighbor. 'He built his fence on my property,' that kind of thing. 'The leaves from his trees are in my yard.'"

"Really? That seems kind of petty."

"Sometimes neighbors don't want to make trouble, as they put it, and they don't call us until things get bad or dangerous, like a broken wall that could fall on a kid. We've got some folks who don't keep their apartments or houses clean, and the folks next door suffer with the roaches and the rats. That's a real problem and we work with the Health Department to try and get those places cleaned up."

Halloran tried not to visibly shudder. "I'm afraid I've seen some of those places. Not pretty."

"No, indeed. We've got vacant buildings that are boarded up and, in tough times like these, you can be sure hobos find a way in. There was a case last year where some jerk built a fire in the middle of a room—can you imagine? On a wood floor. The whole building went up and we were lucky the whole street wasn't destroyed." Bremer splayed out his left hand and, using the index finger of his right, ticked off the other problems they encountered. "Broken staircases in apartment buildings, roofs with holes in them and shingles flying around on a windy day, no heat or water in apartments, electrical hazards, and people setting up businesses in places where they shouldn't."

"Such as…?"

"The guy who decided to set up a metal working shop in a residential area. What? He didn't think the neighbors would mind about the noise. And how many stills and breweries are there in the apartments and houses in this city?" He chuckled. "Maybe those calls go to your department."

"Quite a big task on your hands. These inspectors—the ones who don't do boilers or construction—are they assigned cases as they come in or are they relegated to specific neighborhoods?"

"They have their own patch. There's the map." He pointed over Halloran's shoulder. Turning, he could see the City almost looked like the back wall of a butcher's shop with the designated cuts of meat. "They respond to the calls or letters we get although the calls come into the main switchboard, too, and they send us the messages through the tube." He meant the pneumatic tubes—glass cylinders routed up and down the floors as needed—that ran throughout the building. He picked up one such message on a pink square paper that had lines for a short missive and a telephone number and name attached. "If they have spare time—which is rare, so they say—they might drive around and spot something that is not up to code, stop and talk to the homeowner."

"Do you know if your men have other jobs?"

Bremer tilted his head. "Like what?"

"If they're so versed in the building codes, and I'm guessing many of them came out of the trades, maybe some of them have side gigs. Like house painting or repairs."

Bremer stiffened a bit. "If they do, I don't know about it and it's not my concern. My men work Monday through Friday for the City. If there's a problem on the weekends, the fire department, police or health department call us first thing Monday morning. What my men do over the weekend is no business of mine."

"That's well and good, but I got the impression that Kehoe may have been in the habit of not just suggesting a citation was in the offing but that he could remedy it himself."

"I never heard that."

"Or that he had contacts with contractors or workers who could assist."

"That I had caught wind of. I called him out on it on Friday, as a matter of fact."

Halloran paused, waiting for more of an explanation.

"Someone called in with that insinuation. Now, you weren't in the meeting that the Mayor had with us Friday morning since it was just department directors, but someone had phoned his office about something similar the day before. I don't know if you've been called onto the carpet by the Mayor." He stopped for a bark of laughter. "Oh, he can be charm itself when he wants to. But when he turns those eyes on you, they look as if they could burn through you. And he looked around the room, making eye contact with each and every one of us. You could have heard a pin drop. You can be sure that as soon as I got back here, I gave my guys the same tongue-lashing that I got earlier."

Halloran had his head down scribbling in his notebook and then looked up. "I have an odd question—and maybe you're not involved in this—but an older man, a man who lived in my parents' neighborhood, died recently and nobody knows if he had any family. Are you all involved in dealing with what happens to the house?"

"No, there is a person who works with the court who's called in to try to determine if there are any relatives. If not, a judge appoints an executor, and they take it from there. You could talk to this woman," and here he flipped through a City employee directory, "who could explain the process to you. Ruth Shepherd. I don't know who follows through, but the possessions and house would be sold for the expenses of the burial. More than that, I don't know."

Chapter 11

Halloran got back to the station, drained of energy from an already busy day. No sooner had he sat down than Dominick put his head around the door frame.

"You'll want to hear this," he said, coming fully into the room and making himself comfortable in a chair. "The person who called in on Inspector Kehoe was none other than Mrs. Costello."

"Oh, no," Halloran said, running his hand through his hair.

"Yep, the Queen of Compliance."

"How could Kehoe not know that was her house when he went to shake her down?"

"It wasn't her house. It was her son-in-law's house, so the names are different. He never interacted with her face to face, according to the secretary I talked to."

"Who was that?"

"Nora Gallagher."

"No kidding! Sure, I know her and her family. And she used to work for the Burnsides. Sharp girl."

"Nora is what they call a floater, someone who fills in for whoever is out sick or on vacation and she had what she thought was the good luck to be assigned to the Mayor's office that day. But instead of what she thought would be a glamorous stint, she answered the phone when Mrs. Costello called. Her opening line was, 'I'm Mrs. Eugene Costello. Do you know who I am?'" Dominick laughed. "And the poor girl said, 'You're Mrs. Costello.'"

They both laughed.

"A correct and well-deserved response for an opening line like that," Halloran said.

"Nora seems like a serious girl, and I'll bet she wasn't trying to be cheeky, but it was a ridiculous question. Anyway, getting off on the wrong foot, the woman berated her soundly, telling her how important her late husband was and how since his death she had taken it upon herself to monitor the neighborhood. Judging from the pages of shorthand notes that Nora took, it was quite a lengthy recital. Then she told her the story of the inspector who tried to trick her son-in-law into repairing City property at his own expense. Mrs. Costello might be a pain, but she knows a scam in the making, especially when she saw him take some cards out of his pocket so he could recommend some reliable contractors who could do the work."

"Pretty clumsy work. And trying that in an upscale neighborhood is just stupid."

"Well, it didn't work, and she was watching from a window and got on the telephone right after getting the story from her son-in-law."

"Amateurish, but I wonder why that particular incident got the Mayor so riled up?"

Dominick shrugged his shoulders.

"Kehoe managed to stir up a wasp's nest." Halloran took a piece of paper from his pocket and unfolded it on the desktop. "Bremer gave me this list of the inspectors. Let's get O'Rourke and the other two new guys to help us do the interviews with the inspectors who do the specialized work, so they probably didn't interact with Kehoe much."

"Which doesn't mean there couldn't have been some animosity."

"True." Since they weren't familiar with the inspectors except that first impression earlier in the day, they divided the names on the list evenly among the policemen, and Dominick was tasked with giving out the assignments.

Halloran looked at his watch. "Running late already."

"Where are you off to?"

"Amanda wants a tour of South End. A potential clinic location."

"She's got a lot of energy."

"And not enough everyday experience."

"You're her personal protection person then, not just her chauffeur."

"If you like. Things might have been different if I had given her a briefing about North End rather than Henry

Rogers, who was just trying to impress her with his street smarts. See you tomorrow."

Halloran hurried out of the building to see that Amanda had parked outside the station and was waiting in her car.

"Hello, beautiful," he said, loving it that she blushed at his compliment.

"Your car or mine?" he asked. "On second thought, I'll drive so you can look around. Has the Mayor identified anyone there to be your scout or liaison?" They walked over to his car, and he opened the door for her.

"No, I think Henry is working on it. He said there are so many groups that he's not sure who best to approach."

Halloran looked over at her. "What he's not telling you is that some of those groups are immigrants from very different places who are in distinct neighborhoods and might not get along with each other. Language, customs and religious differences."

"Well, we're all here together in this country now, so we'd better make the best of trying to get along," Amanda said.

"Great speech. Maybe you should run for public office."

"I'm sure you think I have my head in the clouds and that I'm oblivious to how things work. Luckily, I'm not as jaded as you."

He laughed. "Oho! Jaded, am I? You can't work as a police officer, much less a detective, and not be fully aware of the foibles of the real world. I try not to let it affect my personal life, however."

"That's good," she said. "I couldn't bear to be with someone who was too hardened."

Halloran thought that admission was a step forward in their relationship.

"Would you mind if we made a slight detour? I promised Sean I would pick him up from some school activity and take him home. He could get there on his own, of course, but he's got a piano lesson to get to."

"Sure," she nodded.

He turned on the radio and they listened to band music interrupted by commercials about cigarettes and local stores.

"There he is," Halloran said unnecessarily as he spotted his brother waving with one hand while he held a stack of books on his hip with the other.

"Gosh, hello, Miss Burnside," Sean said, sliding into the back seat. "Thanks, Bren. It was going to be a squeeze getting home in time. And Mrs. Foster is a stickler for punctuality."

"No problem, we'll be there soon enough. What did you stay for?"

"Student government. We're putting together suggestions to the principal for reforms."

"Uh-oh," Brendan said. "I didn't know we were harboring a politician in the household. Dad might not like that."

"That's because all the politicians he knows are people he doesn't like. Our generation is going to change all that."

They drove for some time before getting closer to their own neighborhood and Sean called out, "Look! People are working in Old Man Hogan's place," he said, craning his neck as they passed. Brendan gave a swift look and could see that the front door was open, and people were moving things out onto the street.

"Interesting," he said. "I'll swing by after I drop you off." He let Sean out at the curb of his parents' home and, turning the car around, drove back to the activity at the house down the street. "I'll only be a few minutes," he said to Amanda as he got out of the car.

Halloran walked past a young man who was taking a chair down the steps and went into the house that smelled as if it hadn't had a good airing out in some time. There was a sorry-looking chenille sofa with crocheted doilies on the armrests that had seen better days.

"Hello," he called out and a man came out of a back room wiping his hands with a rag.

"What can I do you for?" he asked.

There was an awkward moment where the two of them recognized each other but couldn't place the context. "Don't you work for the City?" Halloran asked.

"Yes, but I'm not on duty. I have an after-hours job of furniture removal. It seems the old man died and had no family, so we're taking this stuff to be sold."

"It doesn't seem to be that long ago that he passed away."

The man shrugged. "I don't know anything about it."

"Wait, what's your name?"

He stepped forward more into the light, a tall man with a smile on his face and innocent-looking blue eyes. "Rick Slater," he said. "At your service." He extended his arm to shake hands.

"Does your boss know you have another job?"

"Shucks, we all do. The City doesn't pay very well, and we all have some experience in the trades. Corcoran has a roofing business, Polchek does landscaping on the weekends. If it doesn't interfere with our workday, the boss doesn't care. And it is after hours," he added, looking at his watch. "What are you doing out after hours?" he asked.

"My family lives in the neighborhood. What happens to all this stuff?"

Slater shrugged again. "The lawyer sells it to pay for the expenses. That's all I know. Hey, watch out, Jack," he called to another young man who banged a chair into the jamb as he wrestled it out the door.

Halloran followed and went back to the car where Amanda was watching the removal process and looking at Slater in the doorway.

"That man is looking at you intently," Amanda said.

Halloran smiled and waved at him. "He's one of the inspectors who works for the City. Poor old Mr. Hogan just passed away recently and they're already getting rid of all his stuff. Or selling it."

"I didn't know the City did that."

"They don't. He's working as a private contractor, from what he told me."

"During working hours?" She turned around to look back at the men struggling to get a couch out the door.

Halloran shrugged. "It's technically after hours. He made it seem like many of the workers have side jobs and as long as it works for his boss and their rules, I'm not going to get in the middle of it."

"Then tell me about South End," Amanda said.

He blew out his cheeks. "In a nutshell? Surely you must have been out of Beacon Hill at some time in your life."

"Don't be silly. Of course, I have, and I've been to South End, too. I meant, what is your impression of it today?"

"Most of it was tidal flats or marshes before they filled it in to extend the City and build those row houses."

"I know that part. One of my father's cousins is an engineer, and he used to regale us with stories of the feats of construction because of the lack of bedrock or something."

"Like many of the neighborhoods in Boston, the makeup of the population changes as new people move in and others go to the suburbs. There have been a lot of immigrants and now people from the southern states are moving in looking for opportunities. If your sister had followed through with her studies in social work, she would have been able to tell you about the settlement houses there. Which, as I come to think of it, would be an excellent location for a clinic."

"I remember the Sons of Italy building was being used for nutrition classes when we had the first clinic in the North End. Isn't it amazing that we think everybody should eat the same foods in the same way as us?"

"Assimilation, it's called. The Harriet Tubman House would be a good location except it is mostly for single women who have come up from the South getting their bearings and who need a place to stay. I doubt if they bring children and probably don't have room for a clinic." He turned left onto Clarendon Street.

"What about the YWCA? Or do you think that's for single women mostly?"

"They've got this big new building," Halloran said, slowing down and pulling to the curb.

"I'll say! I read about it in the newspapers. I'm a bit concerned about approaching an institution with an established board and mission. They might not want to veer off their beaten path. The Mayor suggested a smaller settlement house on Shawmut Avenue. Let's look at that."

Halloran turned right onto Tremont Street, drove a few blocks, turned left on Dartmouth and then onto Shawmut Avenue. "The heart of South End," he stated, driving slowly, and they both tried to locate the building.

"There it is," Amanda said, pointing to a midsize brick building in the middle of the block. Halloran stopped the car, and they looked up at the structure.

"People could certainly find it easily enough and there is public transportation. Do you want to go in and talk to somebody?"

"No, I'd prefer to call and make an appointment rather than burst in on someone."

"Good plan. Where to now?"

"I'd better get back to my car and go home."

He looked over at her and put his hand on her face. "So soon?"

"I'm really tired from today already. And I have a feeling I might have to run interference for Louisa with my parents once they find out what she's been up to."

Chapter 12

Amanda couldn't wait to get to her room and take off her shoes. How did women work all day in heels? She rubbed her feet and reclined on her bed, closed her eyes and relaxed. It wasn't more than a few minutes before she heard tapping at the door and wondered if she shouldn't pretend to be asleep. The door opened quietly and she heard her sister's voice.

"No playing possum—I know you just came in."

Amanda sighed and put her hands behind her head. "No rest for the weary, I suppose."

"I thought the expression was no rest for the wicked."

"Louisa, I have the feeling you are about to ask a favor of me and if so, I would suggest starting out with a better approach."

"Favor? No, I was going to ask you to accompany me to the Oasis tonight."

"I consider that more than a favor. You know Mother and Daddy don't want you seeing Rob Worley or going to a nightclub."

"Come on, don't be such a stick in the mud. It'll be fun. Didn't you enjoy the music and the refreshments last time?" Louisa had turned on her best wheedling tone.

"I could do with a nice glass of champagne."

"See, that was easy."

"In exchange for you taking that box of IOUs back to Rob."

Louisa sat down heavily on the foot of her sister's bed, crossed her arms and scowled.

"You'll get terrible wrinkles making faces like that."

She hit Amanda on the foot. "I should twist your pinky toe for being so devious."

Amanda laughed. "Devious! The pot is calling the kettle black!"

"All right then. Mother stayed home all day and tailed me like some private investigator, so I had a devil of a time sneaking off to call Rob."

"Speaking of sneaking, is that the modus operandi for later this evening? Although your more responsible older sister is very tired from a long workday."

"I hope you're not going to hold that over my head. Just months ago, the notion of one of us working was a shock to Mother. If you keep this up, she'll want me to get a job. Can you imagine?"

"You could model like my friend Marnie at some swanky salon."

Louisa wrinkled her nose.

"I think they give the models a discount on the clothing," Amanda added.

"Well, that's a different thing altogether," Louisa said, perking up.

"Or work at the cosmetic counter in Jordan Marsh."

"Discount or no, Mother would be horrified if I were to be out in public at a department store, as if we needed to work. And I couldn't bear the sneers of my deb friends who would think we're on the brink of the poorhouse."

"Times are changing, Louisa. If Mother doesn't think so, you should."

"Get up. Let me show you some of the new dresses I brought back. That will be my bribe to you."

"Looking at them or getting to borrow them?" Amanda got up in her stocking feet and followed her sister down the hall to see the bounty. Louisa threw the closet door open, and her sister gasped.

"How did you manage to get all those?" She pushed one evening gown after the other past on the closet rod.

"Eunice's cousin got married last year, is very pregnant and couldn't bear to see these in her closet. Aren't they scrumptious?"

"She gave them to you?"

"Yes. None of the other girls could fit into them and her cousin was convinced she'd never regain her former figure before they went out of fashion. What a haul, eh?"

"This is delicious," Amanda said, pulling out a white silk dress that draped beautifully.

"Beautiful tailoring," she added, looking at the finishing on the seams.

"This is so decadent, but they have a servant whose entire job is sewing their clothes and taking care of them. Can you imagine?"

"Oh, dear, Louisa. Is Southern living suddenly appealing to you? What about your cadet? What has he got to recommend himself?"

"Aside from the fact that he is gorgeous, attentive with wonderful Old-World manners, and ridiculously rich—what more could a girl want?"

"I'm guessing you haven't had the conversation with Rob about your Southern sojourn?"

"Not in any detail. Romance-wise, that is. I'm still considering how to play all of this."

"Are you thinking that, if you mention the cadet, you'll induce Rob to make a commitment?"

Louisa turned her attention to the next dress on the rack, avoiding her sister. "It had occurred to me."

Amanda shook her head. "Keep me out of your machinations. I will go to the club with you—although I don't know why—but I will not be part of this ruse with the 'engaged to be engaged' business with the cadet. Either way, someone will get hurt. Now, where is that shoe box?"

MR. BURNSIDE WAS LATE GETTING home, full of apologies as he joined his wife and two daughters in the sitting room prior to being called to dinner. He was all smiles as he kissed his wife and poured himself a small glass of sherry.

"So glad to be home. Held up at the office with someone who came late to the appointment and then loaded all sorts of complications on me."

"Such as?" Louisa asked.

He flapped a hand at her. "Ridiculous lawyerly details. I won't bore you. But, just to let you know, if you should ever be in a situation to need an attorney—although I can't imagine how that might come about—it is essential to tell him every relevant bit of information. I can't tell you how many times the client is standing up, ready to leave, only to say, 'One thing I should have mentioned.' And then we sit down again and hash the whole business out once more with that new information as a factor."

"Do you think they don't imagine those little things might be important? Or is it that they might be embarrassed to tell you everything?" Amanda asked.

"Depending upon the situation, a little of both. But I don't want to talk about that. I want to hear all about Charleston, Louisa. I've barely had two minutes with you since you got home."

"It was lovely. An old city with some spectacular homes on the Battery. That's where Eunice and I were staying. The houses are three stories high, with the second floor able to catch the breezes off the water. Even though it's always warmer than here, it was still chilly, but they said it's very hot and humid in the summer and that's why the public rooms are on the second floor."

"Like some of the old mansions here," Mrs. Burnside said.

"And there are balconies and French doors everywhere with fabulous views of the city."

"You mentioned going to a concert on a Sunday, I remember," her mother said. "Do they have entertainment on Sundays?"

"Yes, in this ancient church down by the waterfront. Someone told me that the steeple can be seen out to sea. It has the queerest wooden pews, as if they were built for little people."

"Folks used to be smaller back then, I suppose," her father said. "I'm sure you've seen those little boots in museums and wonder how people had such tiny feet."

They were summoned into dinner by Mary and continued talking on their way in.

"Did you meet a lot of nice young people?" Mrs. Burnside asked.

"Of course. They had a special tea dance in our honor."

"Goodness," Amanda said. "I guess they thought you were very special."

"Aren't I?" Louisa teased back. "I think they were surprised to see guests from the North. They're very touchy about the whole Civil War thing."

Mary came in, served the dinner then left.

Her father stifled a chuckle. "Yes, I can see how they might be."

"We went out to Fort Sumter, but I think I told you that. The guides used the funniest language, like the War between the States and Our Glorious Cause."

"Well, they lost, and they are prideful people." Mr. Burnside then launched into a long explanation of the causes of the war and the role that his wife's family and his had played in the Union Army. Stopping to take a breath, Mrs. Burnside interrupted.

"Amanda, dear, you look very tired. Are they working you too hard?"

"Not really. I hope I don't look exhausted. I guess I'll turn in early," she said, nudging Louisa under the table with her foot.

"That sounds like a good idea for me, too," Louisa said. "All that traveling is so tiring."

They continued eating and listening to Mr. Burnside expound on Southern politics and the aftermath of the Civil War until he couldn't help but notice the attention of the women in his family waning.

A simple dessert of poached apples with cream ended the meal and the sisters begged off due to exhaustion, dragging themselves up the stairs as if about to tumble into bed. Instead, Amanda followed her sister to her room to choose an evening gown for the club visit since the selection had grown significantly.

"No, you don't. The white silk is mine. I think this green one will look wonderful on you. You know we blondes look terrible in green."

Amanda arched her eyebrows wondering where her sister picked up such notions and held the dress up in front of her and admired the effect in the mirror. "This will do. I'm going to get ready and lie down, completely dressed. If I fall asleep, so much the better to catch up on needed rest. Don't knock on the door, just come in and wake me."

She went back to her room, changed her clothes and applied makeup. Then, like sleeping beauty, she lay on her back on top of the coverlet, turned off the lights and closed her eyes. She had no idea how long she had been asleep before Louise was shaking her shoulder gently to wake her.

"Did you really fall asleep?"

"Yes, and it felt wonderful."

"Are you awake enough to drive?"

"Absolutely. Are the parents in bed?"

"Yes, let's go."

Amanda put on a long wool coat and saw Louisa topping her dress with a fur.

"Where did you get that? Rob?"

"Of course not. I haven't seen him since I got back. Another one of the cousins in Charleston said she was tired of this, and I was more than happy to relieve her of the burden."

"Those people must be filthy rich to give away evening clothes and a fur coat without thinking twice. Not like us frugal Yankees."

"They do have rice plantations, but I think they were trying to impress me, too."

"Have you got the shoebox?" Amanda asked and Louisa grimaced as she held it in her hands.

They crept down the back stairs, through the kitchen and down to the garage level, backing the car out carefully without the headlights on until they reached the end of the lane.

Beacon Hill was quiet as any residential area would be at that time of the night, but traffic increased as they got closer to the city center and then the club district.

Amanda pulled up in front of the Oasis, so named because of its Middle Eastern theme personified by the doorman who wore a flowing shirt, spangled vest and turban. It was an arresting look and a bit ludicrous with the pointed shoes, but at least it told any passerby at a glance what they might expect upon entering. She wasn't sure what country or culture he was supposed to represent, but everyone was aware of Rudolph Valentino's portrayal of 'The Sheik' and the costume the doorman wore fit the theme as most Americans, who had never been to the Middle East, knew it.

He took the keys, acknowledged them by name and drove the car to the parking lot. They were greeted at the door by another, similarly dressed man and deposited their outer garments with the girl at the hat check stall just inside the door. Off to the side they saw José, Fred's brother-in-law, a charming Latin American, talking to a group that had reserved a private room. His attention was diverted by the arrival of the Burnside sisters, and he excused himself to come over and welcome them himself.

"A pleasant evening made even more lovely by the addition of your presence," he said, taking Louisa's hand in his, bowing and bestowing a kiss on it, then repeating the action with Amanda.

"Please, let me seat you near the front," he said, although Louisa was not looking forward to getting glares from Sophia, the songstress who saw the younger woman as a threat. But though the band was playing, she was nowhere to be seen.

"Where is Sophia?"

"No here tonight. Sore throat or something. We're letting her rest up before the busy weekend."

Amanda looked at her sister and, by the look that was returned, it was clear that they both wondered if the absence of the singer was intentional on Rob's part and whether she might have made some inroads with the boss during her competitor's absence.

"Is Rob here?"

"Yes, he is attending to some boring business tidbit. That's what's so nice about being the silent partner although my wife would disagree. She thinks I talk entirely too much."

"How is Caroline?" Amanda asked. "Is she here tonight?"

"No, she has tired of coming so often and chose to stay at home. There is some big news going on in the family. Perhaps you've heard?"

"No, of course not."

"My brother-in-law has found a pleasant young woman and now they are engaged."

"Valerie?" Amanda asked, knowing full well who it was.

"Yes, I take it you and she are friends."

"We had our coming-out together and have been in touch ever since. Well, good for him and good for her."

"Let's celebrate their good fortune in finding each other." He turned and snapped his fingers and a waiter appeared with the requisite champagne in coffee cups as they took their seats. Something caught his eye at the entrance, and he excused himself to greet some newcomers.

"That was fast," Louisa said.

"What, the delivery of the champagne?"

"No, Fred and Valerie's engagement."

"A rebound romance," Amanda said with sarcasm.

"You may joke about it, but you're exactly right."

"That's fine. In my opinion, he had hit the spot in life where he felt he needed to be married and I was the one who was available. I'm sorry if I hurt his feelings, but I'm not sorry I declined. As you can see, he recovered nicely, and I don't think he'll regret his decision. They're well suited and her former boyfriend made her and her family uneasy with his constant shifting of jobs and interests."

There was a loud shout and hooting laughter that came from one of the private rooms, which caused them to raise their eyebrows at the level of noise. The Oasis was a nightclub, but for all its quasi-legitimacy, it had a refined and sedate atmosphere. A few moments later, a young man appeared at the door of the room, which was made of lattice work to fit in with the Mideastern décor, and yelled out, "Garçon!" like some boorish American tourist in a Parisian café.

One of the waiters, a smile plastered on his face, came over to the young man, who clearly had had too much to drink already and received detailed instructions that they could not overhear from where they sat. But he caught sight of them, smiled and started over in their direction.

"Oh, no," Louisa said, trying not to make eye contact.

Amanda thought the young man looked presentable enough in evening clothes, his hair slicked back in the latest fashion, but his arrogance was apparent and off-putting.

"It's Kenny Deegan," Louisa said behind her hand as he wove through the tables. "The Mayor's stepson."

"Ah," Amanda commented, having heard bits and pieces of gossip about the wild antics of the young man.

"Good evening, dear Louisa," he said making an overly dramatic bow in front of her. "And to whom do I have the pleasure?" he asked, looking at Amanda. He was smiling at her in a leering fashion that made her uncomfortable, but she made an attempt to be polite.

"May I?" he said, sitting down abruptly without waiting for a response. He looked around for a waiter and snapped his fingers and one dutifully appeared.

"Champagne all around," he said.

"I'll bring three coffees right away, sir," the waiter answered with a wink and swiftly left.

"Kenny, this is my sister, Amanda, and this is Kenny Deegan," Louisa said.

"I don't think I've ever seen you here before," he said. "The sun and the moon," and he gestured at them as if making a comparison between Louisa's blonde hair and Amanda's darker locks, but somehow the allusion or compliment, whichever it was intended to be, fell flat.

"I've only been here a few times, mostly with my sister. Such a lively place, don't you think? And so atmospheric with the sand dunes and camels and palms."

"Oh, yeah," he said, looking around as if seeing it for the first time.

Amanda wondered if he drank so much all the time that he never noticed his surroundings. She intuited that the conversation was going to be heavy going and so said, "Are you here with a group of friends?" The intention of her question was to remind him that he left a roomful of rowdy young men from the sound of it and perhaps needed to attend to them.

"Just a bunch of my usual pals." He looked around to see where the waiter had gone and when their drinks might arrive.

"Old school friends?" Amanda ventured.

"I could say we went to school together, but not much, if you get my meaning. Doesn't matter what school you go to, and I've been to a few, they're always at you about comportment." He said this last word in a false, fluty voice as if mimicking someone. "What's that got to do with anything. Phony manners."

Louisa looked at her sister under her eyelashes, clearly giving the message of what sort of person this was who graced their table.

"And what school did you attend?" Amanda asked, trying to keep the conversation going.

He twisted his mouth to the side in his concentration. "First, public school. It was terrible and I was always in trouble. Then our fortunes changed, and I was suddenly in private school. That was even worse. "Bunch of snobs. The teachers and the students. I couldn't stand it. Got into fights, but I gave much more than I got from those toffs. Then another school—can't even remember the name now." He laughed. "Oh, yeah. Reform school."

Amanda had the feeling he was going to go on for many minutes more and changed the subject. "And what do you do now?"

"I have my own company."

"That's commendable at your young age," Amanda said, feeling she sounded like some old matron instead of a young woman.

"What kind of business is it?" That was the most obvious follow-up question.

"Real estate, property management and some sales."

Amanda smiled and noticed not for the first time that in such conversations the men rarely asked her the reciprocal question of what it was she did. They simply assumed that she spent her time attending to her appearance, going to clubs and listening to men brag about their lives.

"I work at Mercy Hospital," she said proudly.

"Are you a nurse?" he asked.

"No, I work with the director. We're expanding the clinics for children into different neighborhoods of the City. It's for families that can't come to the main hospital but who might need medical attention and either can't afford a doctor or don't have one."

Neither Louisa nor Kenny had any follow-up questions, and their only comments were how nice it was for her to be doing it.

"Hey," someone yelled from across the room.

Kenny turned to see several of his friends waving to him to come back and join them and he motioned in turn as if calling them to the where he now sat.

"Please, Kenny, we don't want to take you from your party," Louisa said.

He looked around and said, "We could put together some of these tables. Why don't you all join us? They're a swell bunch of fellows."

"We wouldn't dare impose," Louisa said and just then saw that Rob was making his way across the room, all smiles. Now all attention was on him, and they waited until he arrived, embraced Louisa and kissed her on the mouth.

Amanda had never seen them act in such an intimate way and she decided that she would not let Louisa out of her sight for a moment. Not on her watch. Turning, she saw that Kenny had slipped away and rejoined his noisy friends.

"Amanda," Rob said, kissing her on both cheeks in the Continental fashion. "You both look wonderful. Come sit down. I've given José, my not-so-silent partner, the job of being host for the evening so I can devote my time to you." He turned and snapped his fingers and a waiter appeared with the requisite champagne in coffee cups.

"I like these quieter weekday evenings," Amanda said. "And we really can't stay very long." Louisa shot her a nasty look. "We do have a bit of business to discuss with you."

"Oh?" he said. Amanda admired his ability to be so suave and always relaxed. She wondered if he would continue in this vein once he knew what in her mind was the intention of the visit. "May we go to your office?"

"Certainly," he said, looking surprised. It was only then that he noticed Louisa had a box under her arm and she gave him a look that was meant to telegraph that none of this was her idea.

The office was up a flight of stairs where the music below was hardly heard. A man named Aldo stood at the door, acting as lookout or security. A sofa and chairs were across from a desk without any paper in sight. A large window to one side overlooked the room below.

Rob seated them on the sofa and said, "What is this all about?"

"My sister found this shoebox that you gave me and insists upon knowing what it's all about," Louisa said. She handed it to him.

Amanda was impressed at how Rob looked at it as if he had never seen a shoebox before, much less that one, and he opened it carefully and pulled out a slip of paper. He unfolded it and put it aside and continued in that manner for some minutes.

"I'm sure you recognize those," Amanda said.

"Yes, I do."

"And we can probably agree that these are valuable. Not just to you, but to whoever incurred the debts in the first place.'

He nodded.

"And that's why I wanted Louisa to return these to you. By having them in her possession, she has been put in great danger. I'm sure somebody—or various somebodies, based on the scrawls—has regretted being in the position to owe you money."

Rob put the slips into the box and the top back on the box.

"What do you propose?"

"Why, that you take them back!" Amanda said. "They're no business of hers or my family's."

"Just so." He managed a small smile.

"And now, since we have been partners in crime, or whatever, I think you can tell us who those people are who are indebted to you."

Rob looked down, then at Louisa and smiled a bit. "I don't know if I can."

"Yes, you can. You might not want to, but you can," Amanda said.

He waited a few moments and said, "Young men of means who are always strapped for cash. Gambling and other vices eat up their allowance. So, I lend them money."

Amanda waited for him to go on.

"Some are college boys, and they make good their debts when the new semester begins, and their bank accounts are refreshed by their fathers. And other people. Like one man who unexpectedly died, and I should tear his up. Or like the Mayor's stepson, Kenny Deegan, who may never pay me back."

Amanda tried not to visibly react. "That's not a good look for the Mayor."

"No, indeed," Rob said with a smile. "There he is right now, acting like he owns the place." He pointed at the window, and they got up to observe.

"We were graced with his presence for a while, as you may have noticed."

"And he made himself scarce as soon as he saw me," Rob said.

Amanda got up. "Louisa, I'm going now. You are welcome to come with me and if you stay, I'm not vouching for you."

Louisa glared at her. "We just got here!"

"Yes, and our business is done. I wash my hands of all this. I'm not covering for you anymore. You're on your own." Even having said that, Amanda hesitated, allowing her sister to weigh the options. She was pleased to see that Louisa made the wise choice when she kissed Rob on the cheek and followed her older sister out the door and down the stairs to the main room.

"You know I will hate you forever for this," Louisa said.

"You'll get over it. Whatever you chose to do, it's on you."

Chapter 13

The interview times with the inspectors had been set up and the policemen piled in Halloran's car for the ride over to City Hall. He spoke over his shoulder.

"I don't want these men to think that we're not hauling them to the station because they are special in any way. It's because it was easier for us to go there since there is more room and we can get done with one batch while the other is waiting."

"Each floor has several conference rooms that I've managed to book since they don't have anything remotely private in the basement," Dominick added.

"How long should we question them?" one of the recruits named Schell asked.

"The simple answer is, as long as it takes. We want to find out how well each one of the guys knew him, if they were friends or didn't get along, and where they were Saturday and the early hours of Sunday."

"Do you think it was one of them?"

"Who knows. We don't have much to go on since he wasn't living with his wife, who we just managed to track down this morning. No love lost there, based on her reaction on the phone." Halloran turned to Dominick and said, "We'll go talk to her this evening. She said she works until five-thirty."

"Do you think it could have been one of the people he issued tickets to?"

"I doubt it. The fines that department gives out are small unless you're a company that has done something dangerous. In any event, they can contest a citation and take it to court if they disagree."

Halloran had looked at the list of employees that Bremer had given him and assigned the new recruits to the inspectors who did the specialized work of boiler and mechanical inspection as well as the building permit men. His thought was that those men had less contact with the dead man and the interviews would go more quickly and perhaps were less vital. The remaining inspectors who did similar work to Kehoe fell into the second group and Halloran and Dominick would talk to those men.

There was something familiar about the first man who walked into the small conference room and Halloran cocked his head to the side as if trying to sort it out.

"Do I know you?" Halloran asked.

The other man smiled. "Pete Corcoran. Retired cop." He stuck out his hand to shake Halloran's.

"Sure, sure. And you're working here now?"

"Got to keep busy. Also being at home with the wife all day would drive me crazy."

"One lifetime of enforcement would be enough for me," Halloran said.

"Piece of cake here. Often you don't even have to talk to the property owner. Just slip the notice of violation into the mailbox and be on your way. I work alone and that suits me fine."

"How well did you know Kehoe?"

"Well enough. He was a young punk."

"Hardly young."

"He was to me. I knew him when he was tearing up his neighborhood with his buddies, vandalizing and stealing. He did a short stint in reform school for all his bad ways."

"And they hired him anyway?"

Corcoran shrugged. "You'd think with so many people out of work that they would have their pick of the crop. Maybe he knew somebody."

"Interesting. Did you ever have words with him?"

"Me? No. I steered clear of him. That's what I like about this job. You come in, get your assignments for the day, go out in the field and then come back in the afternoon to do your paperwork. That's it. No need to work with people you don't like."

"What about office politics?"

"I don't do politics. If people don't want to get along, that's not my business.'

"Are you saying he didn't get along with somebody?"

"I'm saying I don't pay attention to what people are saying to each other. I close my ears to the chatter and the banter that goes on. Otherwise, I'd never get my work done."

Halloran had expected that an ex-cop would have provided him with some good insight into activities in the bullpen, but it seemed this one just did his job and shut out everything else.

"Thanks for your time. Let me know if you happen to remember something or hear anything."

"I won't. See you."

Halloran shook his head to clear his thoughts at the abrupt ending to the interview before talking to Slater. Earlier in the day, he had called one of his friends in the City prosecutor's office to ask what he knew about the person who worked with properties left by people who died without families and intestate. Bremer had told him it was Ruth Shepherd and she was the liaison between the attorney appointed executor and whomever was hired to do the removal of the furnishings. Halloran wondered how Slater got the removal job in his parents' neighborhood since that wasn't in his inspection district.

A few minutes later, Slater knocked on the open door and came in, all smiles and assurance, and greeted Halloran by name before sitting down.

"Being a detective sounds like an interesting job," he said.

"I guess so. Long hours, though. And sad circumstances, too."

"Yeah, I wouldn't like that. What do you need to ask me?"

"It seems your group of inspectors interact with each other more than with the specialized men."

"The boilermen got that by seniority and extra training. I haven't been doing the job as long as those old guys." He laughed. "They get paid a little bit more because of it."

"How well did you know Kehoe?"

"As much as I know any of the men. He had the district next to mine so I would sometimes see him when I was out and about. Even had coffee with him just last week."

"Did you get along?"

"Sure. What's not to like about him? He was funny."

"In what way?"

"Funny ha-ha, not funny peculiar. That would be Torgan who is mighty peculiar."

Halloran looked puzzled but said nothing, waiting for the other man to elaborate.

"He's very religious and always talking about it. Trying to get us to go to his church. And he's fussy about his desk, always dusting and cleaning it. Anyway, he didn't like Kehoe at all."

"Why was that?"

"He thought Kehoe was disrespectful to Mr. Bremer. And he heard him cussing once and told him off."

"Okay. But back to you and Kehoe. Everything okay between you?"

"Sure. Everything was okey-doke between us."

"I wanted to ask you something else that has nothing to do with the death of Kehoe. I have to say, when I stopped at Hogan's house yesterday, I was surprised to see you…."

Slater interrupted him. "Like I told you, I have a side job clearing out those places."

"Yes, I remember you told me that. I was wondering how you got the job?"

"I heard they were looking for folks to do that, so I applied. It's not skilled labor, you know."

"What happens to the furniture and the rest of the possessions?"

"I don't know. We deliver them to a warehouse and there is some attorney in charge of selling the stuff, I guess. That's what I heard."

"I never thought about it before. Interesting. Where were you Saturday?"

"My day off. I was working on my sister's place doing some repairs. Back and forth from my place to hers to get more tools and the lumberyard."

"In and out of her place all day. That's nice of you."

"That's me all right. Had dinner with her and the family and went home bushed from the long day."

"Do you know why Kehoe was in the office Saturday?"

"Nope. No idea."

"Well, thanks. If you remember anything else that might be important, you know where to find me."

"Sure thing." He looked down at the notebook in which Halloran had been writing and nodded his head before leaving.

Halloran continued to write for some minutes and thought he might need to ask Bremer why Kehoe would be in the office on a Saturday. He had clarified that they didn't work on the weekends. But it was obvious that they came and went by the basement doors so the security guard in the lobby might not know if anyone had been down there.

While he pondered that, he heard Dominick's footsteps approaching in the hall.

"How did it go?" Halloran asked him.

"Nobody knows anything. Everything's fine. The only remotely interesting thing is that Torgan had a low opinion of the deceased."

"So I heard from the guy who just left."

"He's a quirky fellow. Smiling all the time when there's nothing to smile about."

"Tell me about Torgan," Halloran said.

Dominick sat down and blew out a breath. "Rigid, overly serious and determined. Looks you right in the eye and quotes some Biblical verse to back up his statements."

"So, he didn't approve of Kehoe?"

"More than that. He said he told him he was going straight to hell if he didn't mend his ways."

"Phew—that wouldn't be fun to encounter every day at work. Your fellow employee watching your every movement and saying you'll end up in the fiery furnace."

"This may sound odd, but as he was relating it to me, he didn't mean that Kehoe would come to a bad end in life. He seemed to imply that he really would end up there."

"That doesn't mean he would kill him," Halloran said.

"No, but it's a damning thing to say to his face, much less relate to a detective investigating a murder."

Halloran closed his notebook. "Have we done everyone?"

"Yes, the recruits covered two other inspectors and I told them we would have a debriefing back at the station."

"I still want to talk to Kehoe's wife or ex-wife or whatever she is."

On the drive back, Halloran asked the men in the back seat how they thought things had gone. He was looking for a general response, but he heard O'Rourke flipping through pages as if preparing to give his recitation right there in the car.

"We'll get into the details when we get back, but overall, how did it go?" Halloran often liked to engage in conversations in a moving vehicle where eye contact wasn't possible. He felt people were often more relaxed and forthcoming than being quizzed in a formal meeting room.

They each murmured that it went fine, and he could see in the rearview mirror that they were looking for cues from each other as to what to say next.

"Don't worry, when we get back and sit down to a cup of our department's terrible coffee, you'll get right into the swing of things."

It was like every other initial debriefing with new recruits. They were by turns nervous and cocky and intent on how everyone else was doing as if it were a contest. If O'Rourke set the tone with his excessive detail, it wasn't a bad thing although in the end not much new information was revealed.

"Everyone maintains they were either at home or doing something but certainly not anywhere in the vicinity of City Hall late on Saturday. But that's just their word for it. Our job is to get some corroboration from others that their alibis hold up. Knowing that they have access to the basement bullpen without having to go through the front doors of the building means the security people have no idea who comes and goes."

"It is possible that whoever did this is someone that Kehoe had a beef with? Or gave a citation to?" one asked.

"Seeing as how the inspectors were in the habit of propping open the doors when they went out for a smoke, it is entirely possible that Kehoe, a smoker, did so and someone either sneaked in when he wasn't looking or it was someone he knew. It could have been someone he thought was friendly and turned out not to be."

"That opens everything up," Schell said.

"That's true," Halloran replied. "We can rule out a robbery. But aside from that, we don't know what else this guy was up to that may have incurred someone's wrath."

"Can we conclude that it was a man who did this? Based on the method of the attack?"

O'Rourke asked.

"I would lean in that direction," Halloran said. "There was evidence of a physical fight, but anyone with a significant weapon, such as the hammer with which he was killed, could have inflicted some of those wounds and bruises." He could see them all wince as they envisioned the attack.

"By the way, the techs looking at the ashtray couldn't lift off a distinct set of prints. It looks like everybody in the place had their mitts on it at some time. Good work, men. We'll regroup tomorrow after you've done the follow-up interviews and see where we are."

They dispersed with Dominick staying behind. "Do you want me to go with you to the woman's place?"

"It's a rough part of town, but I'll be okay."

Minutes after Dominick left, the Chief appeared in the doorway, always an ominous sign. Halloran stood up but sat down after the Chief waved his hand downward.

"How is the case with the inspector going?"

"We've interviewed his co-workers and will be checking up on the alibis, but this is a tough one."

"How so?"

"Terrible security at City Hall with several points of access where people came and went during the workday and could have access afterhours or the weekend."

"I've been there on the weekend, and you have to check in with a security guard at the front desk."

"Yes, that's true. But there are doors in the basement where the inspectors work to which they all have keys. It's how they come and go from the parking lot without having to go around the building, up to the lobby and then back downstairs. There are a lot of them in and out and who knows who else may have gained entry?"

The Chief shook his head. "Here's my take on it. I've already heard that man was a bad apple—not that he deserved to die. But if we can wrap this up quickly, we can have the Mayor's staff turn their attention to the security issue in the building. I don't want a big deal made of it because everyone will think it's our problem to solve and it's not. It was sloppy work on their part, and they need to fix it. How soon until you can wrap this up?"

Halloran was stunned. It hadn't even been a week and it seemed the Chief wanted to sweep it under the carpet. "I'll see what I can do."

"I know I can count on you," the Chief said and left the room.

After he left, Halloran wondered if he shouldn't have brought up the issue of his odd position of being the functional supervisor of the detectives but without the title. Or the pay. He could have kicked himself for passing up the opportunity of mentioning it. Well, next time.

He shuffled through his notes and wondered if there was something that he had overlooked, and the only thing they hadn't yet considered seriously was an irate constituent. To know who that might be, he needed to look at Kehoe's paperwork or notes or however they logged their business. It was entirely possible that some hothead wanted to contest a violation and decided to do it in person. A long shot, but you never knew. As he was picking up his hat, the phone rang.

"Are you working this afternoon?" Amanda asked.

"Of course. Are you?"

"I have a meeting with the Mayor's aide to talk about some contacts and logistics."

"I'm on my way to City Hall myself. Can I give you a lift?" he asked and agreed to pick her up outside the hospital.

"Hello, gorgeous," he said, opening the car door for her.

"You'd better watch out or I'll get a swelled head," she said.

"I think your head is pretty swell, too."

She laughed and thought back to her days dating Fred, who had never made her laugh.

"I don't know how long I'll be. Why don't we agree to meet in the lobby when we're done? We can get a coffee or an ice cream at that wonderful place around the corner."

"It will spoil my appetite for supper, but I don't care."

He parked down the street. Entering the building, she took the elevator up to the top floor while he took the stairs to the basement. By the look on the faces of the inspectors who were in the bullpen, his was not the most welcome. He nodded to some and made his way to the office of Mr. Bremer, who was equally displeased to see him although he disguised it better.

"I need to ask you a few more questions," he began.

Bremer motioned to a chair and Halloran began. "Is there any reason any of the inspectors would be here on the weekend?"

"No. They work eight to four with weekends off. In the best situation, we would have funds for them to be on call in the evenings, overnight and on weekends but there is no budget for it. So, the fire department or health department —depending upon the issue—fills in for us and we pick up the slack on Monday morning. Busiest day for us."

"Why was Kehoe here, do you think?"

"I have no idea. They all have keys. We can't very well have them turn in their keys at the end of every day, you know."

"Of course. But their ability to come and go from two access points is a problem. He could have brought someone in with him for all we know."

"We typically don't get visitors," Bremer said.

"I'd like to look at whatever cases he was working on. These men fill out paperwork of some kind, right?"

"Yes. I've given his cases to the others to follow up on, but we can sort that out. Do you think it was some issue with a homeowner or landlord?"

"Possibly. I'd like to check."

They went back out into the bullpen and to Kehoe's desk, which was bare compared to the others. Bremer called out to Slater, whose desk was farther away. "Hey, you got some of Kehoe's cases, right?"

"Yes, sir," he replied although he continued sitting at his desk.

"Bring them here," he motioned impatiently.

"Sure thing." He gathered up a stack of papers, shambled over to his supervisor's office and nodded at Halloran.

"Is that all?"

"Yes, sir."

"What do you make of it all?"

Unsure what he was being asked, Slater scratched his head and twisted his mouth to one side as if thinking deeply. "I'm not sure."

"Well, did he have approximately the same number of cases as you?" the boss asked.

"Not nearly the same."

Mr. Bremer waved him back to his desk and looked at Halloran, who was thinking that, if anyone should know how many cases each inspector had, it should be the boss.

"Just so you know, we found several violation warning notices crumpled up and put in the trash. They had Kehoe's name on them."

Bremer pursed his lips in anger. "I had a feeling he was working some angle out there. Maybe one of his victims was trying to get back at him."

Halloran said nothing and looked over the papers that Slater had given him. "I'll need to take these with me. You have carbon copies, right?"

Bremer nodded and remained standing when Halloran left and went up to the lobby to wait for Amanda's meeting to end. He looked through the stack of papers with names and addresses and scribbled notes along the edges whose meaning he could not decipher. He saw the name Brown, the son-in-law of Mrs. Costello, and the date which placed the inspector at the house on Thursday. That made sense from the sequence of events of his boss getting a call and perhaps the call to the Mayor, as well. How did one man's grift cascade into a murder?

About ten minutes later, Amanda exited the elevator with a strained smile on her face.

He waited until they were out of the building before asking what the matter was.

"I never knew the Mayor had such a temper."

"Why was he angry with you?"

"He wasn't. When I got there, he was on the telephone in his office with the door closed, but I could hear him berating someone with most unpleasant language."

"How do you know he wasn't chewing out Henry?"

"Because I could only hear his side of the conversation. His secretary was at her desk in the outer room, and I could tell that she was embarrassed by her cheeks turning red, but she didn't say anything. When things died down, she went into his office and came out shortly thereafter and motioned me in. And there was the Mayor, cool as a cucumber smiling at me from behind his desk."

"Like any politician, he can turn the charm on or off at will. Here's the place," Halloran said, opening the door to a quaint ice cream parlor with its gleaming subway-tiled walls behind the counter. "Booth?" he asked.

"It would be more comfortable, but I want to pretend I'm ten years old. Let's sit at the counter where I can swing my legs." She sat on one of the swiveling chairs with a smile.

The man behind the counter was dressed all in white with a little peaked cap on his head. He recognized the detective and greeted him by name.

"And what'll it be today for you?" he asked placing a napkin to the left of each of them.

Amanda glanced up at the menu board behind him and settled on chocolate ice cream while Halloran ordered the same but added a cup of coffee.

"What's going on with the inspector case?"

"The whole thing is a bit of a mess. The boss there likes to think he's keeping his men in line, but it seems he doesn't have a clue what they are doing. There are some managers who take the time to visit their workers in the field, but it doesn't look like Bremer does. He didn't know what cases Kehoe was working on and asked Slater what the usual case load was. That's something the boss should know. It looks like Kehoe was trying to shake down property owners by getting them to hire someone he recommended to eliminate the violation."

"Do you think it's possible the boss got angry when he found out about it and killed him?"

"We know anyone could have come in through the basement doors and nobody would blink an eye about the boss being there. But he doesn't strike me as someone who would do that. He hasn't demonstrated much energy in relation to the whole thing. But I could be wrong."

The coffee appeared as well as the ice cream in parfait glasses.

"What about some of the people he was intimidating? Do you think someone could have been angry enough to go down to City Hall, find him and kill him?"

"Not according to the security guards' descriptions of how they checked people in. It's unlikely that a member of the public would know where their offices were and try to enter the basement from the outside."

"So, it's got to be someone who has access to City Hall."

Halloran turned to her. "I really wish you hadn't said that."

"Why?"

"Because now we have to go back to City Hall and look at that roster again."

Chapter 14

"You could have at least let me finish my ice cream," Amanda complained as Halloran was paying the soda jerk and putting on his hat.

"Here, put it in a cone. Can't have the lady upset," he suggested to the man.

"Now I feel ridiculous, like a little girl who stamped her foot to get the treat she was promised," Amanda said, taking the filled cone from the man.

As they walked, she asked, "How in the world are you going to narrow down everyone who works in that building and tie him to Kehoe?"

"I might not have to look at everyone," he answered.

The guard nodded to them as they entered the lobby and was surprised when Halloran approached him. "Do you still have the roster from Saturday?"

The guard reached under the counter in front of him and brought out a clipboard and flipped back to Saturday. "You said that someone came in and went upstairs to retrieve his briefcase and came back down shortly thereafter."

"Yes."

"Who was it?"

The guard looked at the sheet and muttered. "Since he said he just had to pick something up, I didn't put a check next to his name."

Halloran exhaled in frustration at another hole in the security system. "Do you remember who it was?"

"Sure. The guy who works in accounting. Elmore Brown."

"Thanks. Was there anyone else that came in who didn't get a check next to his name?"

The guard chewed on his lip. "Here, look, I checked off the Mayor's name. He came in with his son."

Halloran looked up at the guard and stared in amazement at that oversight.

"What? I couldn't check him off because he's not on the roster," the man said in response.

"So much for security," Halloran muttered as he held the door open for Amanda. "Let me drive you back to the hospital."

WHEN HALLORAN GOT BACK to the station, he looked for Dominick to fill him in on the messy recordkeeping at City Hall but couldn't find him anywhere.

"O'Rourke, where is Detective Barone?"

"In an interview room with some woman. She said it was about some inspector."

Halloran shed his coat and hat and found the closed door down the hall and tapped on it. Dominick opened it.

"You'll want to sit in on this."

It was Nora Gallagher who sat opposite and was just as surprised as Halloran.

"I feel outnumbered," she said with a small laugh.

"Miss Gallagher was just telling me about something curious that came to her attention." He let her speak for herself.

"This is not about the inspector who died recently," she said choosing her words carefully. "It's about another one. He comes up to that floor sometimes and talks to Miss Shepherd, who works with the Court on settling estates or something. This is probably none of my business, but it looks like it's more than a business relationship, if you get my meaning."

Halloran waited for her to explain more.

"You know I'm a floater, and this week I'm working on her floor. It's something about requisitions and, because she sometimes wants things done quickly, instead of doing interoffice mail, she asked me to walk it through the several departments. She gave me the envelope and asked me to make sure to tell them to expedite it. I was happy to do it because it gave me a chance to see some of the other departments—I'm not going to be a floater forever. Anyway, I trotted down to accounting, then over to finance and finally to my last stop and when I used the word 'expedite,' the man gave me an exasperated look and said, 'She's always in a hurry.'"

"I saw him write a check for two hundred dollars, then put it in an envelope. He handed it to me before I went back upstairs. I gave it to her, and she closed the door to her office. My desk is outside, but some distance away. A few minutes later, I saw this guy who visits her frequently come out with the envelope in his hand."

She stopped waiting for a reaction and seeing there was none, said, "Don't you see?"

"Frankly, no," Halloran said.

"She gave it to that inspector."

"How do you know he is an inspector?"

"His uniform. It has his name on it. Slater. Tall guy."

They still didn't react.

"I'm confused. What's the issue?" Halloran said.

"Someone explained to me that her job is the liaison with the attorneys assigned by the court to settle the estate of people who die without family or a will. I guess he sells the belongings or something. I saw him give her something in a small bag last week. I think they are in cahoots and selling the dead peoples' more valuable belongings and keeping if for themselves."

"Whoa!" Halloran said. "That's quite a leap."

Nora looked him straight in the eye. "Then how do you explain someone on her salary coming in to work with a gold bracelet?"

"She saved up her money?" Dominick suggested.

"An old-fashioned bracelet."

"Some auntie gave it to her?" Dominick clarified.

Nora shot him a look that said she was nobody's fool.

"He told me that he does this kind of removal work as a side job evenings and weekends and it's on the up and up," Halloran said.

"Don't you think it's odd that he's her boyfriend and he's the only one who does the work? I mean, who knows what he finds in the houses of older people? My gran used to stash money in flour canisters and some people hide cash in the pages of books. Is this man operating on his own with no supervision?"

"Good points, Nora," Halloran said. "But I wonder if you shouldn't take this issue to someone in City Hall instead."

She gave a short laugh. "That would be the end of my job. I thought you could do a better job of figuring out what kind of racket they have going."

Halloran smiled. "It really pays to have someone with street smarts working there," he said. "Another person wouldn't have put it together. What's the woman's name again, Shepherd? I'll look into it."

Nora told him. "And you'd better not make any reference to me, or I'll be out on my ear."

"I won't say how I got the information. You know, someone in my parents' neighborhood died recently and it was exactly that inspector, Slater, tall guy with the wide-eyed look, who was hauling everything away. Who's to say where it went or how much it sold for? Who's to say whether he found something hidden away and put it in his pocket? Just another example of how loose things are at City Hall."

He glanced at his watch and saw it was almost five-thirty. Elmore Brown would be getting back home about this time and Halloran decided to meet him there. He had the address from the crumpled-up ticket and thought talking to him on his home turf would make him more likely to speak up. The roads were still crowded with commuters, and he thought how lucky Brown was to live in that neighborhood with tall elms providing shade in the summer, then wondered if he bought the house from his mother-in-law. Good old Mrs. Costello.

As he pulled up in front of the house, he wondered what had made Kehoe choose this home to ticket and saw the sidewalk crack that hardly constituted a tripping hazard. This affluent neighborhood told Halloran that neighbors were concerned about appearances, and nobody wanted folks up the street to wonder what inspectors were doing on the property. *Make them go away as soon as possible* was the usual reaction rather than in the working-class neighborhoods where the homeowners were happy to engage in a shouting match with the authorities, not just to avoid a fine, but also to demonstrate to the neighbors who wasn't going to take guff from anyone.

Halloran walked up the steps to the porch and rang the bell. A young woman answered the door. He introduced himself, showed his badge and asked for Elmore Brown. Her eyes widened as she ushered him into the living room.

"I'll get him," she said, going out to the hall and up the stairs.

Halloran could hear talking and then the footsteps back down the stairs and stood up to introduce himself to Mr. Brown, a tall, handsome man who looked as if he had only just come back from work as he had shed his suit jacket but still had his tie on.

"What can I help you with?" he asked. His wife came into the room and stood behind his chair.

"I'm investigating an incident that occurred last week. A certain City inspector, Mr. Kehoe, came out to your house and attempted to give you a ticket for some sidewalk repairs. Is that right?"

"Yes. I was surprised because it's been like that for a while, and nobody had mentioned it to me before."

"And did he tell you it needed to be fixed and that you were responsible?"

"Yes," he said.

At that moment an older woman came into the room and stood with her arms crossed over her copious bust.

"I'm Mrs. Costello."

"How do you do?" Halloran said, getting up and offering his hand to shake.

She didn't take his hand. Her eyes narrowed and she pointed a finger at him. "I know what's what in this world, and let me tell you, that skunk was trying to shake us down." She jutted her chin at her son-in-law and said, "He didn't know that it's the City's responsibility to maintain the sidewalks, not us. He figured he could intimidate Elmore one way or the other—either hold out his hand for some cash and if that didn't work, the other famous scheme—that he knew a guy who could make it right. It happens every day."

"I don't know about that—," Halloran began but was interrupted.

"Well, I do. My late husband and I owned a bar back when you could." Here she looked at her daughter, who seemed embarrassed that her mother would boast about such a thing. "Made good money and could have kept more if the cops hadn't been coming in for free drinks or offering protection. You City folks make good money and get a pension when you retire. Why do you think you need to gouge people, too?" Her face had become red.

"Mom, sit down," the daughter said softly.

"I'm not going to sit until I hear what this cop has to say."

"The inspector who was here on Thursday was killed on Saturday, and I am following up with anyone who interacted with him."

Mrs. Costello's shoulders relaxed, and she did sit down and patted the loveseat cushion next to her, indicating that her daughter should sit as well.

"Was there an argument?" Halloran asked Elmore.

"No. I just listened to what he said and when I went inside, Maddie asked me what was going on and then told me that he was out of bounds, and she was going to report him. She took the copy of the ticket that he gave me, so she knew his name and I don't know who she called."

"I'll tell you who I called," Mrs. Costello said. "That bum, Bremer, who runs the inspection department. He doesn't know what his guys are doing out on the street all day. He just sits in that office ticking off the months until he retires. I could tell by his voice that he didn't give a—." She stopped short of saying something crude based on the look her daughter gave her.

"That he would listen to me rant and then do nothing. So, I called the Mayor's office then, too. My late husband and I knew the Mayor from way back and I take it as my civic duty to call him directly when I see something wrong. And I did."

Halloran then wondered what dirt she had on the Mayor besides knowing him, but he let it pass.

"Mr. Brown, you went into City Hall on Saturday to retrieve a briefcase?"

"Yes, yes, I did," he said, looking directly at Halloran, but blinking.

"What time was that?"

He looked at his wife. "About four o'clock, I guess."

"Where is your office?"

"Second floor. In accounting."

"What was so important that you needed to retrieve your briefcase? Wait a minute, wasn't it strange that you should have left it at work in the first place?"

"I was preoccupied on Friday because all the departments seemed to have a meeting about dishonest behavior or something, and I wondered what that had to do with us in accounting. The whole office was abuzz about it. It was unnerving and when I left, a colleague and I were engaged in speculation about it. It wasn't until I got home that I realized I had left the briefcase at work."

"You didn't think to go back and get it then?"

"I did, but I didn't want to face the office, to be honest. To think that someone would think that we might be up to no good was upsetting."

"And yet you had just experienced that very thing when you had come home for lunch the day before. And your mother-in-law made the calls to City Hall that resulted in those accusations."

"I didn't know she had called until Sunday or Monday."

"Did you go down to the basement when you went to City Hall?"

"No, why would I?"

"Because that's where Kehoe was on Saturday. And was until they found his body on Sunday."

"I've never been down in that basement."

Halloran continued to write in his notebook.

"If I had, the guard would have noticed."

"How? There is no indicator above the elevator in the lobby as to which floor anyone is going to. You could have stepped into the elevator and gone to the basement and then back up to retrieve your briefcase. Or even used the stairs."

Elmore jettisoned himself from the chair. "What are you saying? That I killed that man?"

"Just asking," Halloran said.

Elmore looked to his wife and mother-in-law. "Of course, I didn't! I never would. I got my briefcase and came home. Didn't I, honey?" he asked his wife.

"Yes, he wasn't gone long."

Halloran got up. "Well, thank you for your time. I think that clears it up," he said.

Mrs. Costello got up and went to the front door and opened it. "Don't come back again," she said.

Chapter 15

Amanda came home to a quiet house until she reached her bedroom and could hear snuffling noises from down the hall. She tiptoed toward Louisa's room and, peeking through a crack in the door, saw her sister prone on the bed trying to muffle her crying.

"Louisa—what's the matter?" Amanda asked, entering and closing the door behind her.

"Everything's ruined," she muttered with sobs.

"What now?"

"I've found out the worst." She sat up in bed, her eyes puffy and red. "Rob wants to break off our relationship."

"On what grounds?" Amanda asked. She could think of plenty but didn't voice the obvious: Louisa was too young, they had different backgrounds, Rob owned a nightclub, had dealings with bootleggers and might be a loan shark.

"He told me that he had a criminal record and knew that Mother and Daddy would never approve of our continuing to see each other."

Amanda collapsed into the slipper chair in the corner of the room and shook her head. "Is this the first time he told you?"

"Yes, isn't it terrible!"

"The criminal record or that he didn't tell you?"

Louisa burst into tears again. "Both."

"Did he tell you what for? Did he go to prison?"

"Yes, as a young man. For robbery. And somehow Kenny Deegan found out about it."

"Ah, that explains a lot." She saw Louisa's pleading face and tried to soften the blow.

"That's not good. Not good at all. Maybe that was the correct decision on his part, all things considered." Amanda conceded that the end of Rob Worley would solve a lot of potential problems for the Burnside family. Or perhaps just for her.

Louisa glared at her.

"How was he able to buy a club, sign a lease, borrow money with that in his background?"

"You're always so practical. He doesn't own the club. He says José is the silent partner and I guess that's true because he doesn't flaunt it, but José is on all the paperwork for the club although Rob's money is what put it together."

"Where did he get the money from in the first place?"

"I don't know," Louisa wailed. "And I don't think I want to know now."

Amanda went to the bathroom to retrieve a washcloth that she had rinsed in cold water along with a glass of water and two aspirin. "Here you go. The age-old remedy for the weepies. Take this," she said handing over the aspirin and the water. "Lie down and try to sleep. Putting a sleep between you and your latest trouble is the best remedy."

"I'll never be the same," Louisa said, obeying her sister.

"We never are. That's the point."

Amanda left quietly and wondered how much of this she should tell Brendan. Nothing now, of course, but how long should she shield Rob Worley? And did she need to? He had done something wrong in the past but that shouldn't condemn him to life as a pariah. Somehow, he had managed to land on his feet and gracefully at that. But she didn't trust that he wasn't still involved in illegal activities—besides the obvious one of selling alcohol. That she had been complicit in drinking.

While she was turning over in her mind what to do, if anything, about her sister, Halloran was making his way to the home of Kehoe's wife or ex-wife in one of the seedier sections of town. He was by himself but thought that, since he was just getting background on the dead man, he was on safe ground.

The apartment building was brick and looked respectable, with lights visible through most of the windows; it was the darkened buildings that usually put him on alert. The hall was well lit, another good sign, and well swept. He walked up to the third floor, rang the little buzzer with her surname underneath and waited. He thought he could hear someone come softly up from the other side and hesitate. He rang again. The door flew open.

"Whaddyou want?" the large man in an undershirt said, his stubbly chin inches from Halloran's face.

"Hold on, buddy," he responded. "I'm a police detective here to talk to Velma."

The man did not seem intimidated but backed off. "Sorry. We've had some trouble from time to time."

"Is she here?"

"What's this about?"

"It's about her husband."

"Not anymore. He croaked."

"I just needed to get some background information on him. Is she here?"

"Yeah, I'm here." A dark-haired woman with vivid blue eyes spoke behind the large man. "Let him in, Lee."

Lee stepped aside and she motioned with her hand for Halloran to come inside. It was a tidy room but clouded with cigarette smoke. The radio was playing, and she turned it off. Without sitting down or asking him to sit she tilted her head up, blew out a stream of smoke and asked what he wanted.

"You know Kehoe died last week."

"Yeah. Boo-hoo. The guy was no good."

Lee stood to one side of her, just the size of him a threat.

"Do you know of anyone who might want to do him harm?"

She stifled a laugh. "The line would go around the block. He managed to make enemies wherever he went." She took one more drag of the cigarette, removed a piece of tobacco from her tongue and squashed the butt out in the ashtray. She remained standing.

"When was the last time you saw him?"

She looked over at Lee and shrugged her shoulders. "A couple of weeks ago, maybe? He came over to try to get the title for the car. Lee told him to shove off. It's my car now."

"Yeah, the guy was a number one jerk."

"Did you know him, too?"

"Sure, I used to work with him at the City. Some tools went missing, he blamed me and got me fired. With all the shady stuff he was doing, I'll bet you anything he took those tools."

"Was your boss Bremer?"

"Yeah. Same spineless guy. I don't know if they had something going but he went after me and no one else. Good riddance to that job and Kehoe."

"Where were you last Saturday?"

Velma and Lee looked at each other.

"We took a drive to Crescent Beach and then spent the night at my mother's place in Revere."

"Can you give me her address?" Halloran said, taking out his notebook.

"It's not like I write her letters. She lives with her sister. I know how to get there—I don't know the exact address."

"Just the street name would help."

She hesitated a moment. "Maple Street," she said, and he wrote it down, sensing she had made it up. He took a card out of his pocket and handed it to her. "If you think of anything else, let me know."

"Sure thing," she said. glancing at the card.

He let himself out. feeling their eyes drilling into his back as he did so.

Chapter 16

Halloran began the next morning with pulling together the group to review what information they had and where there were holes to be filled. They trooped into a small conference room, each person clutching either a notebook or a file folder.

"All right, let me start by saying this has been a frustrating mess of a case, but we've had some of those before, haven't we?"

Dominick rolled his eyes and nodded.

"And unlike any books or movies you've seen, no one person puts the pieces together and—presto—has a solution. It takes a team. Let's go over what we know. Kehoe did not get many positive reviews from his co-workers. What's your take on what they said? And feel free to jump in with any questions or observations."

O'Rourke looked around the room briefly and said, "I'll go first. The boiler inspection folks said they rarely interacted with him."

"Likewise, the building permits men," Schell said.

"The men who do building permits knew of him, of course, and one said they thought he got under the boss's skin sometimes. But they seem to do very different jobs and didn't come into contact with him too much."

"What about the men he did interact with?" Halloran asked.

"I interviewed Torgan and two others. Torgan is a strange fellow. Self-contained and serious," Dominick said. "He said that he considered his job one of great responsibility to the public and not to be taken lightly."

"Excuse me, sir," Schell interrupted. "What do you think he meant by that?"

"I got the impression that he was trying to tell me something without actually saying it. As we continued talking, he made one comment and then another about Kehoe being without conscience."

"The boss made mention of strong religious feelings on Torgan's part."

Halloran caught O'Rourke looking at Schell with a puzzled face.

"It may be something, it may not, but if the man is a zealot and he thought Kehoe was a sinner, that could be a motivation to do harm."

O'Rourke wrote in his notebook. "That's good to know."

"Jensen is a fairly new hire and was still tagging along with Polchek to learn the ropes," Dominick said. "It's a learn-as-you-go sort of job with very little training. Neither of them said much about Kehoe except he could be a bit of a cut-up."

"What about Polchek?"

"He's been doing the job for several years. One of those guys who keeps his head down, or so he says."

"Each time I questioned the boss he seemed more peeved that his day was interrupted than anything else. He said that Kehoe was a wise guy and that he chewed him out for something on the Friday before he died. But he didn't add anything to flesh out who Kehoe was or how he felt about him," Halloran said.

"Maybe he didn't like to get too personal with the employees," Dominick suggested.

"Corcoran is a retired cop who knows the ropes and decided not to say much of anything. He well knows that the more you say, the more you'll be asked to elaborate. So, he kept his trap shut for the most part during the questioning."

Dominick raised his eyebrows in recognition of that type of reaction.

"Slater was the only one who said anything remotely positive about Kehoe. Their districts were adjacent, and he said they had coffee from time to time. So, what's the thinking about the inspector group as possible suspects?"

The room was quiet as the recruits looked at each other as if to inquire if they were allowed to speak.

"O'Rourke. What do you say?"

"Inconclusive so far. Sir, you mentioned the lax security in the building and the two access points. It could have been anyone."

"Schell, what say you?"

"Based on what you've presented, there's not enough ill feeling. Just my opinion."

Halloran looked at Wilson, the third recruit, who usually barely spoke.

"They said they didn't work weekends, so what was anybody doing there? Not just Kehoe but anybody else? I can't imagine coming in on my day off just because."

That got a laugh, and he turned red.

"Not unless I had to. For work's sake, I mean," he clarified.

"And the boss? Do we think he was still angry enough about whatever happened on Friday to take it out on Kehoe over the weekend?"

"How would he have known Kehoe would be in the office?" Schell asked.

"Exactly!" Halloran said. "I don't think this was opportunistic. It wasn't somebody wandering in from the parking lot through a propped open door and going berserk. It was someone who knew him and who may have made an appointment with him."

"But why kill him there? With people in and out of the building?" Schell asked.

"But it was the weekend and people were not in and out of the building. At least the security guards have said that the building was locked."

"Except for anyone with keys to the basement entrances…," Dominick interjected.

"And the guards have a roster of employees, so they know who comes and goes. Except for at least one person. Mr. Brown. And Kenny Deegan."

The recruits looked at one another, not putting together that it might be the Mr. Brown that they saw in the crumpled citations in the trash pile they had sorted through.

"Mr. Brown is the key to all this. It was he who Kehoe approached and tried to fleece but the mother-in-law caught on and called into either the boss or the Mayor or both, telling of the incident. That's what all the meetings, lectures and dressing-downs were about."

"If Mr. Brown had got Kehoe in trouble, wouldn't that have been enough? And what would he be doing in the building?" Barrett asked.

Halloran pointed at him. "Exactly. But it was Mr. Brown's mother-in-law who got Kehoe into trouble. And, as it happens, Mr. Brown works in City Hall in the accounting department and popped in on Saturday to retrieve a briefcase he had left in his office."

The men murmured at that revelation.

"Once he left the lobby, he could go downstairs and confront Kehoe, get in an argument and lash out in anger."

"But why?" O'Rourke asked. "What's his motivation?"

"Maybe he felt belittled by having almost fallen for the scam and then being shown up by his mother-in-law, a known person in City Hall who calls out whomever she thinks needs straightening out. Embarrassing."

Dominick screwed up his face as if to differ but said nothing.

"Yes, I know, that might not be enough of a motive, but I was the one to talk to him and it seems to me that he is not particularly happy with the living situation. Young wife, newborn baby and interfering mother-in-law."

"Who else is there?" O'Rourke asked since he and his fellow recruits had been tasked with other jobs in the past few days.

"There's an ex-wife, or maybe she was still his wife at the time of death, I don't know."

"Is there some kind of death benefit for widows?" Dominick asked. "There is for police officers, but I don't know about the other City workers."

"Good point. Schell, could you follow up with the personnel department and see if that is true? I had the pleasure of talking to Kehoe's wife or ex-wife yesterday. No love lost there, as you can imagine. Her new boyfriend used to work in the inspections division. He claims that Kehoe got him fired."

Dominick whistled. "There you go."

"Alibi needs checking out. She said they were at her mother's place in Revere on Maple Street, but she couldn't recall the exact address."

Dominick gave his exasperated look. "Maple Street? Come on. She could have picked Elm, Oak or Main Street for that matter."

"Where do we go from here?" Halloran asked rhetorically. "We recheck the alibis and look for any holes. Any questions? No, then get going, men."

Chapter 17

Amanda was so concerned about Louisa that she made the rash decision to call the Oasis and speak to Rob, who suggested that she come down to the club rather than talk on the phone. Although she was bone-tired from work and the emotional impact of her sister's distress, she slipped her shoes back on and, in her mother's absence, let Simona know that she would be an hour at most. She wasn't sure what she was going to ask or say, but she had to do something to break the log jam.

Since it was not yet clubbing time, there was nobody outside the front door and all but a few cars in the parking lot. However, the door was unlocked, and she made her way in past the empty hat check stand and into the club itself. Bright lights were on, and several people were sweeping the floors and laying out clean tablecloths. It looked so sad with no musicians, no Sophia and her torch songs, no cigarette smoke, no clatter of glasses and silverware on plates, no conversation. She stood there unnoticed until she heard footsteps behind her and Rob's calm voice.

"Let's go upstairs," he suggested.

She followed him up to his office, took off her coat and sat on the sofa. He opened a cigarette case and offered her one, but she declined. He lit one and leaned against the desk in his impeccably tailored jacket.

"Well, now you know," he said.

"Yes. Louisa is really broken up about it."

He cocked his head to one side. "Interesting. She was shocked and then mad. Now broken up?"

"I suppose she thinks that has ruined a future with you."

He took a moment to consider that comment. "That's not entirely true."

"Rob, in some ways Louisa is sophisticated and in others she is very young. You were the knight in shining armor who was going to rescue her from a dull, boring existence. Now she's found out that the armor was more than tarnished."

"What I did was long ago when I was young and stupid. It's absurd that youthful mistakes should color the rest of one's life."

"Agreed, but that's how it is."

"You're still steamed about the IOUs, aren't you?" he said calmly.

"Yes. It means someone is indebted to you, which puts you in danger and by extension, Louisa. It also makes me wonder how financially solvent you are."

He smiled. "I'm doing quite well. Don't worry on my account."

They were quiet a few moments, summing each other up.

"The IOUs, by the way, largely belong to Kenny Deegan," Rob said.

"The Mayor's stepson? What in the world is he spending his money on?"

Rob shrugged. "He let slip once that he is helping someone out."

"Like some poor widow or orphan?"

Rob laughed. "I think it is someone to whom he owes money or a favor. Or maybe it's blackmail. I don't ask questions. In turn, the City goes easy on me."

"So that's how it is," Amanda said. She got up and put her coat on.

"It's real life."

"Maybe for some of us. But not for my sister."

Rob's blasé attitude infuriated her all the way home. Is this what her sister wanted from life? A handsome, clever man with a stunted moral compass. She didn't doubt he had plenty of money, most of it ill-gotten, with which he could ably support her, but her old friends would desert her, and her new friends would be all those club folks. A depressing thought.

Amanda trudged up the stairs from the garage, not looking forward to an evening of Louisa's sad face and dramatics. But there she was in the sitting room, looking fresh as a daisy, chatting to her mother. Amanda stared.

"You'll never guess!" Louisa said. "Beau is in Boston!"

Mrs. Burnside had a wide smile on her face.

"Who?"

Louisa let out an exasperated sigh. "Beau. From Charleston. He's staying with Eunice for a long weekend."

"Is that Eunice's cousin?"

"No, silly. He's my cadet—my boyfriend."

Amanda slumped into the sofa.

"Posture, dear," her mother scolded.

"I think I need a glass of sherry," Amanda said, pulling herself upright and making for the decanter and glasses. "Anyone else?"

"And we're going to show him the city tomorrow, isn't it exciting?" Louisa said to her mother, who was enjoying her enthusiasm.

The telephone rang and Simona came into the sitting room to tell Amanda that the call was for her. She recognized the voice immediately.

"Brendan, I hope you have something good to tell me."

"What's going on there?"

"The Louisa Burnside show is now into Act Two, where the handsome stranger shows up to set everything on its head."

"What?"

"I'll tell you tomorrow when I see you. You've been working long hours this week."

"Yes, and nothing to show for it. Just a lot of information, too many opportunities for someone to have killed the inspector but no definitive suspects. A typical case. I was driving through the North End earlier and dropped in on Mr. Rinaldi's religious shop to see how things were going with him. And you'll never guess. Mr. Morelli was there talking very cordially until I appeared and then they both clammed up."

"What do you think that means?"

"I think Morelli was the guardian angel who saved the day for the anti-fascists, after Rinaldi's son was killed, is what. With all his pretense of not being interested in politics, it seems the two of them are deeply involved."

Amanda smiled. "You see, even an alleged mobster like Morelli can have a good side."

"I'm not so sure about that," Brendan said. "Until tomorrow evening, then."

She always felt energized after talking to Brendan and returned to the sitting room to see her sister smiling at her.

"I guess I know who that was," Louisa said. "Oh, Mother, I just had a wonderful idea. Let's invite Eunice and Beau to dinner tomorrow night."

Mrs. Burnside said nothing, probably startled by the new developments in her daughter's life. "I suppose that would be nice."

"I have a previous engagement," Amanda said.

"No, you've got to meet Beau. He's darling. And such wonderful manners." Louisa chattered on and Amanda tuned her out, thinking how much more interesting it would be to just have dinner with Brendan than jump into Act Three of the Louisa Burnside drama in her own dining room.

Chapter 18

Amanda came down to breakfast the next morning to see her father scowling at the newspaper he read.

"Bad news?"

"Not here," he said, gesturing at the morning edition. "What is going on in this house?"

"Oh, you mean Louisa?"

"Your mother is all topsy turvy about some dinner tonight and what I thought about roast beef or how about a turkey. All over a young man? And how many young men is she stringing along?"

Amanda poured some coffee. "As many as she can get."

He rustled the paper back into position and tutted.

"Fortunately, or unfortunately, I have a dinner engagement this evening."

"No, you don't, young lady. You're not leaving me to the heavy lifting all alone."

"Daddy, judging by the long letter he sent her, he will fill the conversational gap. And Louisa and Mother can chatter away with him about all the sites in Boston he will have seen."

Mrs. Burnside came bustling into the breakfast room, patting her hair into place and issuing a brief good morning before sailing through the swinging door to the kitchen.

"And so it starts," Amanda said with a chuckle, imagining the impassioned conversation with Cook about what to have for the grand dinner. She put her thoughts to the appointment she had made with the director of the settlement house about the West End clinic and how best to approach the woman who was known to be formidable. It was very important that she stress she was an employee of Mercy Hospital—which she was—rather than be taken as an ex-debutante dilletante volunteering her time because she had nothing better to do. With that in mind, she had dressed conservatively in a sedate gray wool suit that would speak to her serious intentions. Mr. Barlow had given her some background on the director, Miss Kane, a woman who had been politically active enough to get some of the funding for the new building from the City's coffers. Extrapolating from that information, Amanda could assume that the woman was in close contact with the Mayor and other elected and appointed officials, which was confirmed when she met with the Mayor. She thought back to the minutes before that meeting when he had an angry conversation with someone on the phone. Who was it? She knew he had a temper but was surprised that he could turn it on and off like a faucet.

Mrs. Burnside returned to the breakfast room and sighed. "So much to do. And where is Louisa? I hope she doesn't think she can spring these things on us while she sleeps in."

"I'll make sure to get her up before I go, Mother. Perhaps she can make herself useful by going to the florist and getting a suitable arrangement for the sitting room."

"Good idea," her mother said.

"It will be hard to find magnolias in Boston this time of year," her father muttered from behind his newspaper.

Amanda smiled. "I'm sure the illustrious cadet has had enough magnolias in his life. What more Bostonian flowers shall we expose him to?" she asked.

Her father put the paper down. "Isn't there some plant called Crown of Thorns?" he asked.

"Really," said Mrs. Burnside in exasperation as Amanda got up.

"You know I'm having dinner with Brendan tonight but what if I'm here to greet him and set the stage. Or smooth the waters, or whatever."

"That will be nice," her mother said although clearly preoccupied with all that still needed to be done.

Chapter 19

Amanda checked in at the office and gathered her papers and thoughts before stopping in to say good morning to Mr. Barlow.

"Off to the lion's den?" he inquired. "Or should I say, lioness?"

"She can't be as intimidating as all that, can she?"

"No, I'm just teasing. She's been in the public sphere since forever and doesn't suffer fools gladly. Lucky for you that you're no fool. I'm sure the meeting will go well, you'll be prepared as usual, and the road has been smoothed by many in anticipation."

"You'd better stop, or I'll get overly confident," Amanda said, boosted by his enthusiasm.

Just as he had predicted, the meeting was positive, and Miss Kane was entirely in support of the clinic at her site. All that needed to be worked out was the days it was to take place, the staffing, acquisition of the partitions and gurneys—in other words, just about everything. But Amanda had done this already at the North End site and was confident this location would be just as successful. Her next appointment for that day was having lunch with Nora, the Burnsides' former maid, to check in on how she was faring. Despite many of her ex-debutante friends leading more idle lives, Amanda was boosted by seeing more women in the workplace although some employers were hesitant to hire women when men were out of work. Luckily for Nora, no man would consider being a secretary, so her position was assured.

They met at a busy, inexpensive restaurant near City Hall that delivered the orders quickly, enabling employees to get back to work in less than an hour. The fare was limited and simple, but since Amanda would be having dinner out that evening, it suited her fine.

Nora was already seated at a far booth and waved as Amanda entered to call her over.

"My, look at that beautiful suit," Nora said and then amended her comment. "If you don't mind me saying so, Miss."

"Nora, you need to realize you no longer work for the Burnsides or me, so I am no longer 'Miss' to you. And feel free to comment on my appearance and I'll do the same to you. You're looking well, so I imagine your new job is going just fine."

"I thought the idea of being a floater, as they call it, was a second-rate position at first, but it is a vital one. I fill in when someone is out sick or there is a deadline for an important project. It's also a great way to become familiar with the different departments and divisions so when a permanent spot opens, I'll know where to apply."

"That's wonderful. I'm glad things are working out for you."

A harried waitress asked if they had made their selections and they placed their orders quickly.

"I can't imagine working here at that pace," Amanda said. "Dashing around for a few hours."

"Most of them work what they call a split shift. Breakfast shift, a couple of hours off then lunch, a couple of hours off, then dinner."

"That's a long day. I meant to ask you if you got to work with the Mayor's office at all."

"For half a day last week when his secretary had to make some in-person delivery on his behalf." She stopped speaking and looked at Amanda. "I'm not talking out of school here, but the kindly Mayor has a devil of a temper."

Amanda leaned in closer. "I know! I was in the outer office waiting to meet with him and he was shouting into the telephone. When I was admitted some minutes later, he was all smiles. Maybe he puts on the happy act and the angry act with equal ease."

"That's funny. I never thought of his position as one of acting, but perhaps it is."

The waitress came back with glasses of water and two cups of coffee and left just as quickly.

"Oh, goodness," Nora said, moving toward the wall so that Amanda's body hid her from the rest of the room.

"What is it?"

"Don't turn around, but it's that man that comes into the department and hangs out with Miss Shepherd. He's being paid to do some kind of work for the City, and it pays very well."

"Where is he sitting?"

"In the middle section. Tall man in an inspector's uniform."

Amanda dropped her napkin on the ground and glanced around as she picked it up.

"I've seen that man before. He was clearing out the house of a man who had recently died."

"That's part of Miss Shepherd's job. She works with the attorneys who are assigned to dissolve the estates of people who die without relatives or a will."

"Intestate, they call it," Amanda said.

"How do you know that?"

"My father is a lawyer."

"I wonder who he is with? A very attractive young woman. You wouldn't think someone like him would be so lucky with the ladies, would you?" Nora said. "Not because of his job but because he seems kind of distracted all the time. A bit goofy."

Amanda laughed. "Maybe it's just that wide-eyed look of his. So, tell me, have you been able to use your typing and shorthand skills much?"

"They certainly came in handy when I had to test for the job. Words per minute is what counts but they must be without a mistake. It took a lot of practice to master that."

"I can't imagine," Amanda said.

The waitress came back with their plates and left just as quickly.

"Meatloaf—you may remember that Cook never liked making it. Such a treat for me," Amanda said.

Nora laughed. "They call it poor man's food, but I agree that it is one of my favorites, too. How is dear Cook? And Mary? And the new girl?"

Between bites, Amanda filled her in on the situation at the Burnside home and the quick adjustments that had been made since she left, without meaning to make it seem as if she weren't missed. "You ought to drop in some time and have tea with them."

"Do you think so? It wouldn't be awkward?"

"Not at all. Just be sure to downplay your wardrobe, salary and the excitement of your current position."

"That's funny because there will not be much to downplay now. I am earning more than before, of course, but it was the idea of having a career with advancement that interested me most. And being out among more people."

"And male people, if I'm not presuming."

"You're not. Uh-oh, here comes trouble," Nora said, peeking around Amanda to look back at the main room. "Don't turn around—it's Miss Shepherd and she has just spotted the inspector." She paused a moment. "And now she has just seen the girl he is with."

"I'm sorry to admit it, but I have to watch this," Amanda said, reaching into her handbag and taking out her powder compact and opening it so the mirror was facing the scene well behind her. "Oh, my. Someone is very angry."

What was initially a subversive and silent observation on her part changed as a shouting match began and Amanda abandoned all pretense of not looking and turned around to watch.

"You two-timing—," Miss Shepherd said pushing on the shoulder of the inspector, who was still seated. That action made him stand up and the argument got more vicious and louder, ending as she slapped him across the face. He stood stock still and, for good measure, she tipped the young woman's plate of food onto her lap. The dining room, recently a bustling, noisy place, went silent and then reacted with shock at the action.

"What are you all gaping at?" Miss Shepherd said, looking around the room, and stormed off.

"Holy cow!" Nora said and she and Amanda, like the rest of the diners, watched as the inspector brushed the food off the young woman's skirt, took her arm and escorted her toward the exit. Not too quickly, they noticed, in case the other woman was waiting outside to continue the fight.

"Hey! Hey!" the cashier near the door shouted. "You forgot to pay."

"We didn't get to finish eating," the inspector responded and walked by the cashier, who was unable to take further action since she was trapped behind a counter with other patrons waiting to pay.

"Gosh, there are other City employees here, I recognize some of them. How is she going to face going back to work after that scene?" Nora said.

"I haven't mentioned some of the things I've seen to my parents since I started at the hospital, but I think this will make an interesting story for my dinner date this evening," Amanda said.

Chapter 20

Amanda wouldn't be the only one with a story to tell. After Miss Shepherd left the restaurant, furious and embarrassed but intent on vengeance, she walked to the police station and asked to talk to someone about an important issue. Many of the detectives were out to lunch, but Halloran was establishing the work schedules for the next few weeks and had decided to wait until one o'clock to leave. A knock on his door interrupted his concentration.

"Some woman is here, and she wants to talk to somebody. Right now," the officer said.

"Do you know what it's about?"

"Right now, she said."

Halloran grumbled, pulled on his suit jacket and went out to the reception area to see a woman breathing heavily as if she had run there. Her degree of distress worried him, and he wondered if there was a medical condition to consider.

"May I help you? I'm Detective Halloran," he introduced himself.

"And I am the woman scorned," she said. "Miss Shepherd to you."

He thought he recognized the name although it was not an uncommon one. "This way," he motioned and as she proudly walked down the hall, more than one person's eyebrows were raised at her passage.

Halloran opened the door to one of the interview rooms and she sat down at the small table with him opposite. He reached into his pocket to take out the small notebook and a stubby pencil.

"Is that all the police department can afford?" she asked him, looking at the writing implement.

"I leave my gold-plated fountain pen at home."

It looked as if she was about to make a retort but thought better of it. "I have some important information and I would like some immunity."

Halloran scoffed. "That would depend upon the information. And I haven't heard anything yet."

"I'd like a lawyer."

Halloran exhaled. "I can't just snap my fingers and get someone for you."

"I know a couple of lawyers. Let me call one of them."

"All right. There's no phone in here, let me get you to one." He escorted her down the hall to an empty office, let her in, closed the door and waited outside, able to see her through the glass window set in the door. She seemed calm, but once she saw him observing her, she turned her back to continue the conversation as if he could lip read. It was over in a few minutes, and she hung up the phone and came out of the room.

"He'll be here shortly," she said.

"If you don't mind waiting in the interview room, I can bring him to you when he gets here. Name?"

"Carling," she said, and he didn't recognize the name. At least it wasn't some known gangster's mouthpiece or a pettifogger. He led her back to the first room they had been in and let the front desk know whom to expect and retreated to his office to continue the roster.

Almost forty minutes went by before he got a call that the attorney had arrived, and he left to greet him and get the measure of the man. Early middle age, well dressed and seemingly not surprised to be at the police station.

"She's in there. If what she must share is that important, take a few minutes to plot your plan of attack," Halloran said with a smile. "Then let the front desk know when you're ready." He went outside and looked for the hot dog man who had a cart halfway down the street. Not his first choice for lunch but it would keep his stomach from rumbling during the subsequent interview and make him less cranky. A hearty dinner with Amanda waited, and since it was not yet two o'clock, he suspected that he'd be done with this woman in no more than an hour.

Back in the office, he saw the attorney standing in the hall waiting for him. "She's ready."

Halloran sat down and saw the lawyer nod to his client, and she began her story.

"I work for the City and part of my job is liaison with attorneys at the court who are assigned to resolve what's left when someone dies intestate and without heirs."

"How did you get that assignment?"

She looked over to the lawyer, who met her eyes but did not say anything.

"Judge Woodward recommended me for the position. He knew me because I had worked as a clerk in the court some time ago."

Halloran did not ask how he knew her but was willing to let her go on.

The lawyer interrupted. "Before we get into details, I'd like some assurance that she has immunity if she gives evidence."

"I can't do that because I don't have a clue what she has to tell me."

The lawyer got up and looked at his client as if to encourage her to do the same, but she wavered.

"I'll tell you some of it and then we'll see if we can make a deal."

"Fine by me," Halloran said.

"Part of what I do is contract with someone to do the inventory and then someone else to do the removal and finally another for the sale."

"What happens to the proceeds?" Halloran asked.

"It goes to the state."

"It's called escheat. Unfortunate word," the lawyer said.

Halloran waited for her to continue. "I work with a company owned by Mrs. Murray." She paused. It was a common name and Halloran didn't react.

"The Mayor's wife."

"Ah," he said. He made a note of that.

"Then the removal men come in take the stuff away. If the decedent owned the dwelling, the court appoints a separate real estate person to proceed with a sale, et cetera."

"And let me guess who one of the removal men is. Slater?"

She visibly reacted to that but did not say anything for a moment. "How do you know?"

"I saw him in action recently. And what happens to what he removes?"

"It's supposed to go to auction and that handoff is his responsibility."

"Wait. You're in charge of everything up to that point and then he lets the attorney know when he's got everything ready."

"That's right."

Halloran continued to write then looked up. "What's the issue?"

"I suspect that Slater has been pilfering from those houses."

"What makes you say that?"

"I could say I had a feeling when I saw him flashing twenty-dollar bills, and then he brought me a bracelet, an old-timey kind, sort of fussy. He said it was in appreciation for giving him the work."

"Do you have the bracelet with you?"

"Of course not."

"If Mr. Hogan didn't have any living relatives and that's where it came from, who would know?"

"Exactly. Nobody."

"Did Slater bid for the contract?"

She looked at him blankly. "We don't have a contract per se. It's more of an agreement." She looked at her lawyer, who maintained a placid demeanor.

"Who has authority to make that agreement?" Halloran kept his voice calm so it wouldn't sound like an accusation.

"I do. It's how it's always been done."

"Does he charge by the job or by the hour?"

"I go out to the site with him, and we look together, and he gives me an estimate. Because I have seen the place, I know that's what's reasonable."

"Aside from the bracelet and flashing money around, what makes you think something dishonest is going on?"

"He let slip that he rents a place where he stores *stuff*, as he put it."

"You think that is indicative that he is taking some of the items for himself or for resale?"

"That's exactly what I think."

"Do you have any idea where that might be?"

"Yes," she said, reaching into her handbag and taking out a piece of paper. "He left this receipt in among a stack of papers he submitted for payment. That's what got me thinking."

"Was the bracelet in payment for you giving him business?" Halloran asked.

"No. It was because he thought I was his girlfriend."

"Were you?"

She paused. "In a manner of speaking." She looked at him steadily.

"Does he know that you know about the storage place or garage or whatever it is?"

"No."

"Does he know that you came in here today?"

"No."

"Do you feel safe knowing what you know?"

"I'm not sure. Others are probably involved. But I know a safe place to go until this blows over."

"You'd better let your attorney here know where that is. We don't want you disappearing entirely."

She gave a wry smile. "I still have a job to go to."

Halloran got up and thought: *Maybe for now you do.* Addressing the lawyer, he told him to make sure to get the contact information of where she was going to be before he told her she could go. And he would hold the attorney responsible if she went missing.

Dominick was waiting outside Halloran's office when he returned. "What's up?" he asked.

"Something interesting that may or may not be related to Kehoe's death. In any case, Bremer's crew were an enterprising bunch. And very busy. I've got an address I want to check out. Do you have tools in the trunk of your car?"

Dominick hesitated. "Yes. Will that be in lieu of a search warrant?"

"Heavens, no! We're going into a neighborhood that is well known for break-ins. As we drive by and happen to see that someone's property has been breached, it behooves us to look inside to make sure there is not additional damage." Halloran put his hat on and said, "I'll tell you all about our visitor on the way there."

It wasn't too long of a ride to the address that Miss Shepherd had provided where the speculators had bought up what used to be single-family homes and divided them into apartments. The garages, and in some cases the old stables, were all padlocked and were not for the use of the tenants, who likely didn't own cars anyway.

"I knew someone from this neighborhood. His parents lived on the first floor, and they rented out the second and the attic, too. Gave them enough income that the old man didn't have to work," Dominick said.

They found the address on the receipt, which was a two-story house on a small lot with a little yard in the front and shrubs just coming back to life after the long winter.

"Maybe the homeowner rents out to Slater," Halloran said.

They went up the steps and saw three nameplates and pressed the one that looked the most weathered. Hansen, it said. They could hear a distant bell behind the door and after a second ringing, footsteps approached.

An older man opened the door, wearing pants, an open shirt and suspenders but no tie.

He didn't speak but looked up over reading glasses at the two men, a newspaper in his hand.

Halloran introduced himself and showed his badge to the man, who was alert and on the defensive.

"What's this about?"

"Do you own this house?"

"Yeah. So what?"

"Do you rent out a garage or shed?"

"Yeah."

"A guy named Slater. Tall guy."

"Yeah."

"We'd like to take a look inside that unit."

"It's locked."

"Can you supply the key?"

"He's got the key."

"I'm afraid we may have to break the lock."

"What's this about?"

"We had a report that there may be stolen goods stored inside."

"I don't know nothing about that." He stood there looking at them until Halloran gestured with his hand as if to indicate that they needed to see it. "All right," he said, taking his glasses off and putting them in his pocket and placing the newspaper on a small table inside the hall.

"Be right back," he shouted to someone in the house. Then he led them to the path on the side of the house adjacent to an unpaved driveway and a two-car garage at the back of the property. Each side had two doors that opened outward and were secured by chains that encircled the handles and clasped with a sturdy lock.

"He rents this."

"We'll need to open this up," Halloran said and looked at Dominick, who went back to his car and returned with bolt cutters. The owner's eyes grew wide looking at the tool.

"I don't give permission for you to do this. But if you must, I won't stand in your way."

"That's right," Halloran said with a smile and Dominick applied the bolt cutters; the chain was severed quickly, and he threaded it out of the handles.

"Open Sesame," he said, pulling open the doors.

They stood in awe for a few moments.

"It's like Ali Baba's cave," Dominick said.

The garage was only one car's length deep, but it was packed with sofas, lamps, tables, chairs that hung from nails on the walls, boxes full of china, glassware and silver.

Halloran whistled. "Let's open the other side." Dominick applied the bolt cutters again and swung open the doors of the other unit. It, too, was full of furniture and household items.

"I believe that is old man Hogan's sofa that I saw only a few days ago," Halloran said, pointing to the dingy couch with the crocheted armrests.

"Why is he hoarding all this stuff? You'd think he'd want to sell it as quickly as possible, yet this looks like several years-worth of acquisitions."

"Maybe he was too busy collecting and didn't have enough time to get rid of it. I think Mr. Slater has some explaining to do," Halloran said. "Not a word to him," he added to the homeowner.

As they walked back to the car, Dominick asked if they should pick up Slater right then.

Halloran looked at his watch and said, "He may not still be at work. I think those guys knock off about four o'clock, so he'd be gone already. This can wait until tomorrow. And I've got a dinner date I don't want to be late for."

Chapter 21

Amanda got home to a house bursting with preparations—a new floral arrangement in the sitting room, Mary dusting the already impeccably dust-free furniture, and loud noises from the kitchen that she hoped wasn't Cook tossing the pots and pans about. Simona got to the front door as Amanda approached, her tight mouth and widened eyes speaking of tension.

"Is everything all right?" Amanda asked.

"Oh, yes, Miss. Just a lot of commotion and activity for the grand meal."

"Is it going to be grand? Well then, I'm certainly upset that I shall only be dining in a restaurant."

Simona stifled a giggle and continued through to the kitchen.

Amanda looked around for her mother and found her in the breakfast room, turning the pages of a book.

"Mother, what are you doing? Shouldn't you be getting ready?"

"Looking to see if I can find out about this Beauregard's family."

"What book is that?"

"Marquis Who's Who."

"Goodness, I didn't think we had become such snobs."

"It doesn't hurt to know these things. Your father has put out word to his network of people to see what they know of this young man's family."

"What I picked up is that they are old money Southerners and, while that may be moonlight and magnolias to Louisa, they might not be so happy about a liaison with a stodgy New England family."

"Stodgy! What a thing to say about us!"

"Only in the sense that as a region, we're known to be cerebral and tight-fisted. They're known for being gracious and open-hearted. Discounting slavery and the Civil War, that is,"

"I just want to get a sense of the young man. Louisa is over the moon about his visit."

"She was the same way with Rob Worley," Amanda reminded her mother.

Mrs. Burnside looked up at her daughter. "What about him? I hope he is not still in the picture."

Amanda sighed. "I really don't know. Maybe Beau is the new thing."

"He is not a *thing*," Louisa said from the doorway. "He is a delightful, well-educated gentleman. And if you look further, Mother, you'll see that he is from a good family, too."

"I'm sorry that came out wrong," Amanda said. "I just hope you're not going to tire of him when he goes back home and then break his heart."

"So now I'm a heartbreaker? You're the one to talk. Fred Browne is still moping around since you broke things off with him."

"That wasn't my intention. First, Fred is a moper. Second, he seems to have rebounded very quickly with Valerie. So, my conscience is clear regarding him."

Louisa sniffed and turned her attention to her mother. "What are you wearing for dinner tonight?"

"Oh, is this going to be a formal event?" she asked.

Louisa exhaled. "Yes, I thought that was obvious. They're more formal in the South and I do want to make him feel at home."

"I think the blue silk will be just fine," Mrs. Burnside said.

"And you?" Louisa asked her sister.

"I'm not staying for dinner. I have a prior engagement."

Louisa stared at her sister.

"I'll be here when he and Eunice arrive and chitchat before Brendan comes to pick me up."

Louisa gave a heavy sigh of exasperation.

"Does he have a sense of humor?" Amanda asked.

"Of course. Why?"

"Do you think he would find it funny if—."

"No! Stop tormenting me." Louisa stamped her foot on the floor, which only made Amanda laugh.

"I'm sorry. I'll make myself scarce until Prince Charming arrives and will behave myself impeccably thereafter." She couldn't help but chuckle a bit at the prospect of Louisa's discomfort.

The grand arrival happened at six-fifteen and even behind the closed door of her room on the second floor, Amanda could hear the excited chatter of Louisa and Eunice and the lower hum of a male voice. She checked herself in the mirror, fluffed out her hair and applied lipstick.

Mr. and Mrs. Burnside were standing in the sitting room, smiling and talking to the guests as Amanda came down the stairs. Her sister shot her a look of concern and then, seeing she hadn't put on a strange disguise as a joke, smiled broadly. Following her gaze, Beau turned to see what she was looking at.

Amanda had referred to him as Prince Charming and he fit the bill perfectly. Tall, handsome, light brown hair streaked with blonde from outdoor exercise, he smiled a set of perfectly aligned white teeth. He even wore a military uniform just as Prince Charming had been depicted in the illustrated book of fairy tales that her mother had read to them as children.

"This must be your lovely sister," he said in a lilting Southern accent.

No wonder Louisa had been bowled over by this young man.

"Yes, my dear sister, Amanda," she said.

Amanda greeted Eunice with a kiss and shook hands with the cadet, who not only took her hand, but bowed his head and clicked his heels. Amanda could see her father's eyebrows shoot up and hoped she wouldn't laugh out loud.

"How nice to meet you. I understand you've had a tour of our fair city on the hill."

"Yes, how enlightening to see some of the places where we broke the shackles from Great Britain much as we tried to prevail with our Glorious Cause."

That stopped the smiles briefly and Mrs. Burnside, coming to the social rescue before her husband reacted, said, "I don't know if you imbibe, but we have some sherry purchased years ago—totally legally—and stored in the cellar, if you'd like a glass."

"Thank you. I don't usually take alcohol, but since you offer something so rare, I would be delighted."

Mrs. Burnside looked to her husband, who stepped over to the console where it was stored as she gestured for everyone to sit down while Beau made sure the women were seated first before assisting the man of the house. Louisa looked at Amanda triumphantly and rightly so. The man had impeccable manners if somewhat antiquated political views.

As Mr. Burnside inquired further, it seemed that Beau was in his third year at The Citadel and was not sure if he wished to pursue a military career. As the only male in his family, he said that there was an expectation that he assist them in their holdings, as he put it.

"And what might those be?"

"Our family has been in rice production for several generations and has more recently expanded into other forms of agriculture."

"Like cotton?" Mr. Burnside asked.

Beau gave a short chuckle. "No, my father has acres of daffodil and narcissus plants."

"How nice," Mrs. Burnside said, imagining how pretty they must look and then considering that they must specialize in selling cut flowers.

"As you may know, they grow from bulbs and after they bloom each year, they produce additional bulbs. We sell the bulbs to nurseries nationwide. My father even had a railroad spur installed on the property to transport them to market more quickly."

"Do you live in Charleston or out in the country?" Mrs. Burnside asked.

He had the good sense to look abashed when he said, "We have a house in town but also property in the country."

"The train goes from Charleston to their plantation," Louisa said.

"Very handy when I want to pop home for the weekend," he added.

Amanda suddenly got the full picture of his family's wealth and could see the attraction for Louisa, even supposing she found him charming for himself.

"And you have sisters, is that right?"

"Yes, two older."

"They each have their own house on the plantation property," Louisa said.

"We call it the farm," he corrected her. "It is a farm, actually. Cows and sheep. Corn and timber."

The doorbell rang, and Simona appeared from a back room and answered the door to admit Brendan. She took his hat and coat, and he shook hands with Mr. and Mrs. Burnside and then around the room, never having met Eunice before and pleased to meet the mystery man.

"May I get you a small glass of sherry, Mr. Halloran?" Mr. Burnside asked.

"Just a small one, thank you. What a jolly group you are. I see that you are a cadet, Mr. LeConte."

"Yes, a junior."

"Must be nice not to be a plebe anymore."

"Actually, they called us first year cadets knobs because of the shaved heads that made us look like doorknobs."

"Oh, no!" all the women cried out.

"It's a tradition of hazing the new men. West Pointers call their folks plebes, as in plebian."

"Charming," Mr. Burnside muttered.

"If you don't mind me asking, sir, but are you related to our General Burnside?"

"I don't know if Louisa told you, but our family has been in New England from the first time they set foot on American soil."

"You've never been south of the Mason-Dixon line?" he inquired with a smile.

"Not yet."

The room became quiet for a moment until Beau picked up the conversational baton. "And Mr. Halloran, what is it that you do?"

"I'm a police detective here in the city of Boston."

Beau held up his hands dramatically. "Then I'll be sure to behave myself while I'm here."

That got a laugh and Brendan managed a smile although he had heard that joke many times when first introduced. He looked at his watch. "I'm so sorry to leave on short notice, but Amanda and I have a reservation for dinner shortly that was difficult to obtain, and we wouldn't want to forfeit it." He stood up and Amanda did as well.

"I hope to see you again soon," Brendan said and shook hands all around then went toward the foyer and helped Amanda into her coat before putting on his own hat and coat.

They were quiet until they got to the street and Brendan said in an exaggerated Southern accent, "May I help you with your car door, Ma'am?"

"Thank you," she responded in the same patois. "I don't know where those darned servants are when you need them."

"Phew," he said as they pulled away. "That was strange."

"You know my father is a history buff and the notion that someone would assume he is related to a Confederate general does not sit well with him. That poor young man has many hurdles to overcome if he wishes to ingratiate himself with my father."

"First, let's not refer to him as 'that poor young man.' He sounds anything but."

"He has a house in the city and one in the country. Louisa may have hit the jackpot."

Brendan looked at her. "If it's a jackpot she was looking to get."

"I believe that is exactly what she was looking for."

They rode in silence toward the seafood restaurant that was so popular that securing a spot was not easy.

"I'm glad you could get us in," Amanda said.

"It was a wild day today, but I managed to find a few minutes to get to the telephone. Luckily some other party had canceled."

"What was going on at work?"

"The plot thickens." He said no more at that moment, waiting until they were seated at a harborside table."

"And…?" Amanda prompted.

"I can't tell you very much."

"Then you shouldn't have brought it up. I, however, had lunch with Nora and she filled me in on some of the intricacies of City Hall. And then, you'll never guess what."

"What?"

"I can't tell you very much," she said with a sly smile.

"Touché. But I can tell you're dying to tell me."

Amanda leaned forward. "I am. We went to that busy lunch place near City Hall. You know that man that was clearing out the house in your family's neighborhood when we drove by?"

"Slater?"

"Is that his name? Well, he was having lunch with a young lady and then a woman came in and approached them and caused a scene." Before she could go on with her story, the waiter appeared, and they placed their order of shrimp for Amanda and bass for Brendan with the traditional baked beans and brown bread.

"What happened?"

"She called him a two-timer, dumped the girl's lunch in her lap and left."

"Oho! What time was that?"

"Shortly after noon, why?"

"Because she came in the police station not too long after to tell us an interesting story."

"Now don't tell me you can't tell me any more about it."

"I can't. I'm sorry. But tomorrow I have asked several people to come to the police station so we can review the case." He paused for effect. "And those people are the likely suspects."

"Brendan, if you don't let me sit in on that meeting, I'll never speak to you again." She glared at him.

"What possible justification is there for you being present?"

"Wasn't I there with you when you went to the scene in the first place?"

"Yes, but—."

"And haven't I seen some of the suspects in the course of driving around with you?"

"True, but not all of them."

"Well, who are the others?"

Brendan hesitated and said, "I'm only giving you this information because you are a witness of a sort." And before the food arrived and all through dinner, he gave her his thoughts of what might have happened that weekend.

When he had finished and parried all her questions, she said, "I think I know who did it." She reached into her purse and took out a small piece of paper and wrote a name on it, folded it and gave it to him.

"Put this in your pocket and don't look at it until you've got the person in the bag, if that's the proper terminology. I'll sit quietly in an adjoining room listening in."

"Highly irregular," he said.

"That's me, all right. Breaking all the rules. By the way, I can't wait to tell you what I have in mind for my next career." She dug into her dessert and couldn't see the look of mixed astonishment and apprehension on Brendan's face.

Chapter 22

Amanda never expected to come home to a household in total turmoil, but she could sense the tension before hearing a door slam upstairs and her father's resigned exhalation as he sat in his favorite chair in the sitting room.

"What now?" Amanda asked, still in her coat as she stood in front of him.

"Time for a medicinal remedy," he replied, going to the cabinet where the sherry was stored. Bending over and reaching into the recesses, he pulled out a decanter of whiskey.

"That bad, eh?" she asked, slipping out of her coat, hat and gloves.

"How was your dinner with Brendan?"

"Fun, delicious and informative. He's working on a case that I have some involvement with and he's homing in on the perpetrator."

"Sounds interesting. Is he able to share what he knows about ongoing cases?"

"Not really. No names or details, of course. But being intuitive as I am, I can guess who he might be referring to."

"Ha!" her father said, smiling at her as he poured two short glasses of whiskey. "Now you're going to be a detective."

"What would be wrong with that?"

His head spun to face her. "Why, everything, of course. You'd have to be a policeman—er—policewoman and I don't think there are any of those just now. The notion that a woman would then become a detective is—." He stopped short.

"Ridiculous?"

"I didn't say that. I was going to say, difficult, if not impossible, given how things work."

"But what would you think if I were to become a private investigator?"

He handed her a drink. "I need to sit down. Tonight has already been entirely too much."

"Let's table the discussion of my ambitions and talk about what went on here."

"What was your impression of that young man?"

"Wealthy, privileged, handsome, expecting to get whatever he wants."

"That's it in a nutshell. But, and it's a big but, he's also the most narrow-minded young person I have ever met."

"Really, in what way? By the way, Daddy, you did an excellent job hiding this whiskey from all of us."

"Sometimes needed in times of distress. Your mother prefers the pills that the doctor prescribed." He took a sip.

"You didn't lure Beau into a political or historical discussion, did you?" she asked, knowing full well that he had.

"I wouldn't use the term 'lure,' but the young pup kept making ridiculous statements about 'Glorious Cause' and the 'South shall rise again' and some mumbo-jumbo about how they were terribly wronged and needed to reclaim their place in the world. Why, you'd think he was some ninety-year-old rebel veteran reminiscing about his days of glory rather than a twenty-year-old in the twentieth century."

"I hope you didn't use the term 'rebel,' Daddy."

He harumphed. "As the conversation got more heated, I may have done so."

"Was that Louisa's bedroom door I heard slam as I came in?"

"She's in tears again. As is your Mother."

"Why is Mother upset?"

"The political discussion was the start of it all. What was infuriating was that condescending smile on his face as he attempted to educate me on the failings of the federal government to right the wrongs of Reconstruction that left it to the states to do it themselves. You know, of course, that he is referring to illegal activity and intimidation that has been perpetrated in the South. He had the audacity to speak slowly as if I were not just uninformed, and stupid, but also deaf."

"And Mother was trying to bring the conversation back to mundane things to no avail."

He gave a laugh. "She tried, bless her. She asked him to tell us about his people, thinking she'd hear about his family. He took it another way, outlined his lineage and then talked about the people who were sharecroppers on their plantation—pardon me—farm, as he euphemistically referred to it. 'The people whose families have been with us for several generations.' He was talking about the descendants of slaves without ever uttering the word."

"Of course, I knew that had to be the case based on what he had said earlier, but still it rankled. As the meal was winding down and the conversation became more stilted, your mother thought to take things in a more neutral area and asked about the churches in Charleston, you know, based on the information that Louisa gave us about attending a concert in an old church. And he blurted out that, although his family had been Huguenots originally, they were now Roman Catholics!"

"Oh, Daddy, don't be so old-fashioned. Religion doesn't make such a big difference anymore when people are thinking of marriage."

"Are they? Is she?"

Amanda stammered. "I—I don't know. But why else should Mother have had such a reaction to his religion?" She thought about Brendan's family's religion, which she had never mentioned to her parents and now wondered what kind of reaction that might cause. If their relationship ever got to that stage.

"Your mother is anxious to get your sister settled and this young man seemed so promising, even though he lived so far away. She wanted to get her out of the clutches of Rob Worley and that whole shoddy nightclub business. Although I admit he seems a nice enough fellow in many other ways."

If only he knew, Amanda thought. "She was hardly in his clutches, Daddy," Amanda said. "She willingly pursued him once he had made several overtures."

"The thought of a wholesome young man from a wealthy family to whisk her away from that environment put your mother in a spirited mood. Then, after the political discourse or, should I say, jargon, the religion revelation ruined the evening. Eunice and Beau left shortly thereafter, your mother and Louisa got into an argument, then they both came at me because they insisted that I had baited the young man. Everyone is angry and upset." He paused to take a sip of whiskey. I hope you're not upset with me."

"Of course not. I don't have any bombshells to drop. Not yet at least."

Chapter 23

Halloran called Dominick into his office the next day and shared his plan. The other detective stared at him in disbelief.

"Are you trying to get fired?" Dominick asked.

"I read somewhere that it's easier to ask for forgiveness than for permission."

"It may be easier to ask. But that doesn't mean it's easier to get it."

"Good point. But if I do float this idea of mine, you know that someone will stand in the way. All the way up the chain of command."

"True." Dominick rubbed his chin while he thought. "Are you asking me to come in on this with you?"

"Don't worry. I'll take full responsibility. It could be the beginning of a new chapter in my career. Or the end of it. Let's get the front desk moving on making some phone calls." From his desk he took a piece of paper that had names and telephone numbers on it and said he would make the first call himself.

Although Dominick appeared to agree—or at least didn't disagree—he was still wary. But he took the sheet of paper and left to set things in motion, nonetheless.

Halloran called Bremer's office and told him that he would be there at two o'clock and to make sure his entire staff was there. He could tell the man was curious but didn't press for answers.

For the first time since the idea had come to him, Halloran was feeling that creeping sensation of doubt, but he shook his head from side to side as if to dislodge it. He put his hand in his pocket and felt the folded paper that Amanda had given him and smiled. Taking a breath, he called her at her office in Mercy Hospital and let her know that he would see her that afternoon and sensed her excitement even though she tried to sound casual.

He hadn't even made it to lunchtime when the Chief sauntered into his office in his casually menacing way.

"Sir," Halloran said, standing up.

"You've been a busy boy today," the Chief said.

He had eyes and ears everywhere and someone had leaked the plan.

"My one question to you is, do you know what you're doing?"

"I believe so, sir."

The Chief continued to look steadily at him. "You know I don't do politics," he said, although Halloran knew the man was adept at traditional and back door politics. It was in his blood. "This Mayor let me continue here instead of appointing one of his cronies because he said—and I believe him—I was the best man for the job. And I have proven myself so. Should he no longer be Mayor for some reason, I firmly believe that I will continue as Chief because of my spotless reputation. Other people may not be so lucky. So be careful. Be very careful." He gave a small nod and left.

HALLORAN AND DOMINICK got to City Hall well before two o'clock and took the elevator down to the basement. The tension in the room was palpable and Mr. Bremer, who had agreed to using his space for this assembly, looked none too happy about it. Nonetheless, he greeted them pleasantly and offered the use of his office.

"That won't be necessary," Halloran said. He walked out into the bullpen and felt all eyes on him. "I asked to meet here because it was easier bringing other people here than transporting all you folks somewhere else." He took off his coat and hat and asked if he could borrow someone's chair. One of the inspectors came forward with a straight-backed wooden chair and Halloran sat down. Dominick scoured the room for additional empty chairs and determined they would have enough for all those others who were invited.

As the minutes ticked by, people started drifting in. Miss Shepherd, whose office was upstairs in the same building, walked in, head held high and making no eye contact with Inspector Slater. Elmore Brown came in, looking angry but also nervous, and found himself a seat. Amanda came in shortly thereafter and went to Bremer's office and sat down. He looked quizzically at Halloran, who nodded his approval. Bremer likely thought she was a secretary brought in to take notes and paid her no attention after that initial glance. Minutes passed before Velma, Kehoe's ex-wife, and her boyfriend appeared, getting scowls of recognition from Bremer and several of the inspectors.

Looking at his watch, he saw that it was eight minutes past two and he wanted to get started even though someone had not come in yet. Halloran stood and began speaking.

"You know how some public speakers say, 'And now a man who needs no introduction?' Well, every one of you has met me and, although you might like to forget it, I'm Detective Halloran and this is Detective Barone. I've decided to take an unorthodox approach today and have asked all of you here so I can relate the details of the case and see if we can figure out what happened here."

"Hey, I saw them do this in a movie once," Slater said to a ripple of laughter in the room.

"So did I," Halloran said. "And with this number of suspects, I thought it might be effective."

As he uttered the word 'suspects,' glances flew across the room, some people looking more uncomfortable than others, but at last he had their full attention.

"What we know is that Inspector Kehoe was here on Saturday although we still don't know why. He was killed by a blow to the back of his head, and it looks like he was in a physical fight with someone."

At that moment, Kenny Deegan breezed in, slightly out of breath as if he had trotted there.

"Welcome. Please have a seat," Halloran said.

Kenny smiled, but it was not aimed at anyone. He pulled a chair around and straddled it, his arms resting on the top.

"We just started. Here's what I know so far. All of you inspectors have duties that take you out of the office for the greater part of each day. Some of you have specialized tasks like boiler installation inspection or permit review. Others do more generalized work and Mr. Kehoe was one in the latter group. A curious sequence of events occurred last Thursday. Mr. Kehoe went out to Mr. Brown's property while Mr. Brown was home for lunch and told him that the sidewalk needed repair." At this he could see some of the inspectors making faces of disbelief.

"Yes, you all know that is not a citizen's responsibility; however, it seems Mr. Brown believed he needed to comply. During the conversation, Mr. Kehoe suggested that he knew of someone who could assist in the repair and gave Mr. Brown a business card." He heard someone snort and saw another inspector shake his head. "Mr. Kehoe knew that when the work was referred to his friend —probably at an inflated price—he would get a hefty portion of that. What Mr. Kehoe didn't know was that Mr. Brown's mother-in-law is Mrs. Costello, a politically active woman who knows her way around. Once she got wind of what almost happened, she called Mr. Bremer here to complain. She also called the Mayor's office and let him have a piece of her mind. The Mayor called a meeting of the department directors the next day and gave a lecture about making sure that City employees were being honest with his constituents. When that harangue was over, department directors similarly gave the same lecture to their employees. Mr. Bremer knew exactly who had begun this series of events and he gave Mr. Kehoe a piece of his mind."

"As I see it, at this point, we have two people who are not happy with Mr. Kehoe. Mr. Brown and Mr. Bremer." Both men were about to protest, but Halloran cut them off. "But wait, there's more."

"Inspector Torgan overheard the conversation between his boss and his co-worker, and he was gravely disturbed. As a man of strong principles and a religious man, he was horrified at what he heard. Was he also angry? Maybe. Someone has been harassing him for a long time. Messing up his desk and leaving dirty postcards in the drawers to embarrass him. Was it Kehoe? Was Inspector Torgan angry enough to get in a fight with him? Angry enough to kill him?"

"That's against the Fifth Commandment," Torgan said in a steady but stern voice.

"Yes, we know that."

"Excuse me, but what am I doing here?" Kenny Deegan asked with a puzzled smile, holding his hands out in appeal to the others, certain that they couldn't help but agree with him.

"In due time," Halloran said. Those few inspectors who had been standing got the hint that this was going to take longer than they had anticipated, and they sat down with resigned faces.

"It seems that many people were not happy with Inspector Kehoe. Certainly not his ex-wife, who did not speak of him in kindly terms. Also, not Lee, a former co-worker who claims that he was wrongly accused of something and fired because of Inspector Kehoe's accusations."

"Come on, now. Are we going to rehash that again?" Bremer asked in a weary voice.

"You know he had it out for me for a long time," Lee said.

"Don't trot out that lame alibi. Maybe you should have stayed away from his wife."

Lee stood up and pointed a finger at Bremer. "You should have known that guy was crooked and tried to pin the blame on me. You had no right to fire me from a good job."

Bremer waved his hand in dismissal and Lee was about to lunge in his direction, but Velma pulled him back. "It's not worth it," she said, and he sat down slowly, still glaring at Bremer.

"What about Inspector Slater?" Halloran asked and the man in question shrugged his shoulders as if the question was preposterous. "Good time Charley. No threat there, right? I've learned that many of you have other side jobs, mostly on the weekends." He referred to his notes. "Landscaping and roofing. Inspector Slater has an interesting side job. He helps Miss Shepherd here with those properties left behind by people with no relatives and no will." Miss Shepherd finally looked at Slater with narrowed eyes.

"Well, he *used to*," she said.

Slater stood up. "What do you mean?"

"Our agreement has been terminated. I've found someone else. More trustworthy."

"You can't do that."

"I just did."

Bremer said, "What are they talking about?"

"Part of Miss Shepherd's job is finding someone to remove the contents of the apartment or house. Were you aware that Inspector Kehoe wanted in on the action? Did Inspector Slater tell you of his interest?"

"I don't recall," she said, batting her eyelashes at him.

"You know your way around this building, and you know that you can get in through the basement access. You could have come in that way on Saturday and killed Inspector Kehoe and slipped back out. Even if someone saw you, they wouldn't be surprised. And the guard upstairs would have no record of it."

"Do you think I got into a fistfight with a man?"

"No, he could have got that from someone else. Someone who came in with you. You could have done the coup de grace."

"I don't even know what a ballpeen hammer is!" she protested.

"I don't recall ever mentioning that to you as the murder weapon."

"Somebody must have told me," she muttered.

"But back to your job. You set the process in motion by having Slater and his moonlight job clear out the dwellings and—this is where Mr. Deegan comes in—transfer them to a company that can auction off the stuff."

Kenny nodded.

"D and M services, right?"

"Yes, that's it."

"You and your mother, Mrs. Murray, operate it."

"Yes."

"The Mayor's wife."

All eyes focused on Kenny who managed to keep his composure. "My mother," he said as if that made it all right.

"Only you noticed recently that you weren't getting quite as many jobs as you thought. And when you asked Miss Shepherd about it, she, too was baffled. She had just processed two properties in the previous week, and another was in progress. Where was the stuff?"

"I left two messages with your mother telling her that we had the stuff in storage, but she never called me back," Slater said.

"I don't believe you," Deegan said.

"That's interesting: I was just out at a garage in one of our neighborhoods where Inspector Slater does not store his vehicle but instead a vast amount of furniture and other household goods."

"What are you talking about?" Slater said with his wide-eyed look.

"Mr. Hansen, the property owner, was there when we looked inside the garage."

"That's breaking and entering," Slater said.

"It's his property even though you rent it. And I wouldn't be so quick to accuse someone else of wrongdoing, Inspector. I had a look at your bank account, and it was very robust. No living paycheck to paycheck for you. I suspect that you became acquainted with the habits of lonely, isolated older persons who keep hold of precious items for nostalgia's sake. And who probably have cash hidden in unlikely places that we have all come to know—between the pages of books, in the tea caddy, in a cigar box and let's not forget under the mattress. I think you did a very thorough search of each of those properties before you brought your crew in. You didn't want them finding the goods before you got to them. By the time the crew was ready, all that was left was the furniture, china and knickknacks. I could even give you the benefit of the doubt that you were storing all those things we found in the garage for D&M to pick up later, but I suspect you were going to sell the good stuff yourself and leave them the dregs. You had unlocked the secret of where old people hide their valuables and you've made yourself a tidy sum. Not to mention that you were probably doing much of that removal on City time."

"Prove it!" Slater said.

"I think you fill out timecards, is that right?" Halloran asked Mr. Bremer.

"Yes."

"We don't have to do this now, but later, we'll check if Inspector Slater was supposedly on duty late afternoon Monday when I saw him emptying the house of the recently deceased Mr. Hogan when I happened to pass by."

Slater looked to Halloran and Bremer and back again. "My crew was there. I was on my way back to the office here and I just stopped in to make sure things were going all right."

"We'll check," Bremer said.

"So, what does this have to do with Inspector Kehoe? And what was he doing here on a Saturday outside normal working hours? I think he was here to meet somebody. By pre-arrangement. Now, what has bothered me from the beginning is that the security in this building is terrible. Despite the illusion of safety with a security guard in the lobby during working hours, somebody after hours until midnight when the alarm is turned on, you inspectors can come and go through two basement entrances with your keys, and nobody would be the wiser."

"On that Saturday, Mr. Brown happened to visit City Hall to retrieve a briefcase he left behind on Friday. The guard said he wasn't too long in retrieving it. But there is no indicator above the elevator to say if he went up to his office or down to the basement. All we know is that he was in the building and left. And he never did say what was so important in that briefcase that he couldn't leave it there one more day. Did he go down to the basement and confront Inspector Kehoe for humiliating him?"

"That's ridiculous!" Brown said, standing up, his face red in anger.

"The guard said that someone else was in the building on Saturday. Mr. Deegan, who came in with his stepfather. Why he came into City Hall, we do not know. Again, he could have slipped down to the basement, argued with Inspector Kehoe and lost his temper as he is wont to do."

"Why on earth would I want to kill him?" Kenny asked. "I didn't even know the guy!"

"That's not exactly true. Inspector Kehoe was tired of his small-time schemes to make a few dollars off unsuspecting citizens. He caught wind of Inspector Slater's larger operation and wanted in. Slater told you that someone else wanted a slice of the juicy pie you had to yourselves, and you weren't having any of it. You could have been the person to pop down during your visit with your stepfather and cosh Inspector Kehoe on the head."

"I didn't!" Kenny protested.

"But someone else had access to the basement. Miss Shepherd works in the building and knows the situation down here where people come and go with ease. If you didn't experience it yourself, you certainly heard about it from your boyfriend, Inspector Slater."

"Former boyfriend, if you could even call him that," she corrected him.

"But I can't see you wielding a ball peen hammer on Inspector Kehoe. And you didn't have a motive to do so unless you were acting on behalf of or protecting Inspector Slater."

She scoffed. "Not a chance. Not then. Not ever."

"I think the person who had the most to lose was Inspector Slater. He had hoped, in alerting Kenny to someone trying to horn in on their scheme, that he would do something, but he didn't take the bait. Slater was about to lose the goose that laid the golden egg, and he knew that Kehoe just wanted a slice of the action with none of the work or consequences. You lost your temper; you pushed each other around and came to blows and then you hit him with the hammer."

"I did not. I wasn't here. And you can't prove it."

"We can prove the ballpeen hammer from your work toolkit is missing. Your sister wasn't even home on Saturday when you supposedly came and went from the hardware store in your magnanimous effort to assist her. Yes, she said you had supper with them, as you told me, but she was gone all day."

"That proves nothing!"

"I think the circumstantial evidence is one large step towards getting a confession from you," Halloran said.

Dominick got up and the ominous sound of handcuffs was heard. Slater's wide-eyed look became one of abject fear and he pushed past the others and made a run for it. What he didn't know was that several policemen were outside the bullpen waiting for someone to bolt and they caught him as he ran out the door protesting all the time about his innocence.

Chapter 24

It was only when the detectives and the police had left that Amanda came out of Bremer's office and quickly walked toward the exit with a small, smug smile on her face. The group behind her was in noisy conversation and she hoped no one would ask what she was doing there. Bremer stood with his hands on his hips momentarily debating whether he should, but then thought he had had enough for the day. Kenny Deegan was busy fanning Miss Shepherd, who looked as if she was about to faint. For a woman who had seemed so self-assured, the realization that she had been consorting with an alleged murderer had hit her hard.

Mr. Brown slipped out and, once in the men's washroom, pulled a flask out of his pocket and took a deep gulp. He had thought many times since Inspector Kehoe tried to scam him how he would retaliate and the fact that someone had made it seem as if his thoughts had been turned into the actions of another. It was nowhere near five o'clock, but he was going to tell the boss that he was feeling sick and go home immediately.

Lee walked up to Mr. Bremer, nodding his head. "I told you that guy Kehoe was no good. But nobody would listen. And then Slater had his own scheme going. How about taking me back?"

Bremer said nothing for a moment.

"I know the job, no training necessary. You're down two guys and I need a job," Lee said, adding, "Sir."

"Come in tomorrow and we'll talk." Bremer turned and went into his office and looked for evidence that the young woman who had been in there had taken notes or shorthand, but everything was as he had left it.

The other inspectors were still running over the evidence that Halloran had presented and, although many of them had side jobs and were not averse to cutting corners for the sake of making more money, the audacity of Slater's scheme was a shock.

"Remember when we went out to get something to eat and all he had was a twenty? Who carries around twenty-dollar bills? I knew there was something fishy about him from the get-go," one said.

"Shifty eyes, always vague about where he had been and where he was going. Geez, when this hits the papers, people are going to come down on us like a ton of bricks."

"As if they haven't already. Remember the Mayor's speech that started it all."

"Nah, it was Mrs. Costello who started it all."

"Well, the Mayor's family has its own operation to account for." The inspector who said this was looking at Kenny, who had overheard but pretended not to.

"Are you well enough to walk?" he was asking Miss Shepherd, who by then had regained her color. "I'll take you back to your office."

She nodded her head and they left to take the elevator back to her floor.

HALLORAN KNEW it would be a long day since Slater kept maintaining his innocence and even crying at one point and offering his mother's life as evidence that he was sincere.

"What do you want to bet his mother's not alive?" Dominick said.

They questioned him for a few hours, let him rest, thinking that they had nothing on him, and then brought him back out of his cell and started again. He even began to accuse his sister of somehow being the cause of it, then Miss Shepherd, who he said didn't pay him enough.

"Anybody else you want to blame?" Halloran asked.

Slater thought it was a legitimate question and wrinkled his brow searching for a lifeline.

"Back to the cell and we'll be talking to you in a short while. We're stepping out for a bite to each next door."

"Don't I get anything to eat?" Slater complained.

"Sure, they'll give you something. Take him away," Halloran instructed the police officer who stood at the door.

The two detectives went to a diner a few blocks away and had strong coffee, which they knew they would need if Slater was going to keep up his innocence routine. They ordered the daily special: ham, scalloped potatoes and carrots. While they waited, Dominick spotted an evening newspaper that someone had left behind and flipped toward the back pages to check the sports scores.

"Look at this!" he said, showing Halloran a small piece reporting the arrest of a City employee in the death of a co-worker.

"How did they get the story so fast?"

"It's not much of a story. No details."

"That reporter, Gleason, will come snooping around tomorrow, looking for those details."

"I just hope Slater figures out that holding out is not going to help him much."

They took their time finishing their coffee and trudged back to the station to hear that Slater was anxious to talk to them.

"I'm going to wash up first," Halloran said, not wanting to dance to the tune of a suspect. Taking his time, he also went to his desk to see if there were any messages. He picked up the phone and called Amanda's home.

She breathlessly answered. "How is it going?"

"Slowly. He's Mr. Innocence. I'll be here for some time, I'm sure. But how about a late breakfast tomorrow, my treat?"

"That sounds wonderful. Don't forget to look in your pocket," she said before hanging up.

"*The paper!*" he said to himself and dug it out, opened it and shook his head with a smile. She had written 'Slater.'

The man himself was now in the mood to confess but claimed he stopped in at the office just to pick up some tools and Kehoe was there. He said the smaller man demanded to be let in on the house removal jobs and, when he was refused, attacked Slater. He didn't remember hitting him but maintained that the other man fell and must have hurt his head that way. And no, he didn't know who stole the hammer out of his toolbox.

"It was self-defense! The guy was a sneaky rat, and he threw the first punch. A sucker punch. That tells you what kind of a lowlife he was."

As Dominick was writing furiously to get every word down, Slater kept going on and on about all the humiliations he had suffered while working for the City, the indignities he had borne—although in coarser terms—and still pulled his weight no matter whatever else he was involved with. He finally ran out of breath and started to cry.

"And I gave Ruth all my attention and even a portion of what she had paid me and that's the thanks I get. She ratted me out, too, didn't she?"

"Yes, she did. We checked her bank account, too, and there was way more in there than the salary she pulled down."

"Do you think she'll lose her job?" Slater asked.

"What do you think?" Dominick replied, looking at him with disdain then deferred to Halloran.

"It's very likely."

"Oh, man," Slater said. "This has been the worst thing ever."

Chapter 25

Amanda and Brendan met for breakfast at the diner where he had had dinner the night before. The waitress who was about to get done with her shift looked at him and said, "Do you ever sleep?"

"Gee, do I look that bad?" he replied as she poured coffee for them both.

"Were you pacing the floor all evening waiting to find out if Slater would confess?" he asked Amanda.

"There was more drama at my house. You characterized your family's household as chaos. You have no idea what that means. Louisa was in best form. Still carrying a grudge against my father for baiting the handsome Beau and one against my mother for having pulled the religion information out of him, she wasn't content to pout in her room. No, she made herself very present in the sitting room, glaring at us all."

"What did you have to do with it?"

"My sheer existence as a family member, I suppose. Anyway, after all the histrionics, she announced that she was meeting him at Eunice's house because he was leaving the next day. We breathed a sigh of relief thinking that at the least she would be out of the house for a few hours, which did occur. She was remarkably composed when she came home and said that they had resolved things and she realized that they weren't meant to be and had returned his ring. It turns out he wasn't supposed to bestow it on anyone in the first place, so fences were mended."

"She sounds more exhausting every day," Brendan said.

"And it probably means she'll be back to Rob Worley. But tell me about the aftermath of your Hercule Poirot moment yesterday."

"Who?"

"The detective in those novels where they assemble the suspects and one by one pick them off until they get to the heart of the matter."

"You mean it's in a book? I'm disappointed to know that. I thought that was my own original, brilliant idea."

"Nothing new under the sun," Amanda said as the waitress delivered their order.

"I suspect there will be more fallout from this entire thing. Stricter oversight of what the inspectors are doing every day, restrictions or limitations on outside work and where they can do it. They can't be doing repairs on properties that they have flagged for violations. That's a conflict of interest. Miss Shepherd will probably lose her job."

"Do you think so?"

"That entire loosey-goosey agreement that she had with Slater is suspect."

"The agreement she publicly cancelled yesterday."

"Exactly. I'm sure she should have gone through some sort of procurement process. You can't just give a non-contract contract to whomever you choose. And by the way, as we were checking bank accounts, it looks like she was getting a kickback from Slater."

"So, more than an old-fashioned gold bracelet?"

"Nora was the one who had observed suspicious activity between Shepherd and Slater. I told you that, didn't I?"

"No! That was an important clue you forgot to tell me."

"As Gleason digs further for dirt on governmental malfeasance, he will uncover the obvious work that D&M Enterprises, or whatever they call themselves, is the wife and the stepson of the Mayor. It remains to be seen if that's going to get buried or if it will be me who gets buried for shining a light on it."

"Oh, dear. That would be terrible."

"I could always enter the priesthood."

"You'd better not."

"I may have to. I still don't know how the Mayor knows that we've been seeing each other. I wouldn't put it past him to withdraw his support from the clinics you've set up."

Amanda put her fork down and looked him straight in the eyes. "My first question is, how does he know about us?

And the second question is why would he punish me for my association with you?"

"That's how the world works, my dear. Who holds the cards and when they play them. You can bet your bottom dollar that the Mayor would never resign over such a thing. In fact, if we keep it quiet, it could be to our advantage."

"No, Brendan, don't be like them. Tit for tat. Blackmail almost."

"We'll see." He looked at her with a smile. "But the big question is, how did you suspect Slater?"

"You mean, how did I know it was Slater? You may follow the facts but, in my heart, I knew there was something dishonest about him. That whole wide-eyed innocent act when you looked at him but when you turned your back, he was calculating what you knew."

"You only saw him one time."

"Twice," she corrected him. "And of course, woman's intuition," Amanda said.

"In my line of work, we call it a gut feeling."

"Wherever in your anatomy it registers, people give off sensations and others are adept at picking up on them. That's why, if I come to the end of my job setting up clinics for Mercy Hospital, I may set up my own private investigation business."

Brendan dropped his fork on his plate and stared at her. "Please tell me you're joking."

"No. Why not? I have an inquisitive mind, a dogged need to find answers and nothing else to fill my time. I'm coming into some money so I could rent a little office. Help society women with finding out what their daughters are up to, look for stolen goods, work with the police on the odd murder investigation." She smiled.

"I believe you're out of your mind!" Brendan said.

"And just think, you can be my inside man if I need any information on the sly. And if the Chief ever decides to get rid of you for insubordination, you can come work for me. Wouldn't that be fun?"

A quiet Christmas on Cape Cod disturbed by a murder.
Then a vicious ice storm cuts off contact to the outside world and Amanda may be forced to find the villain alone.
Find it here:
CHRISTMAS MURDER IN HYANNIS
Sign up for my newsletter for updates and more titles.
www.Andreas-books.com
See the entire series:
MASSACHUSETTS COZY MYSTERIES
If you enjoyed this book, please let other readers know. Reviews help readers discover my books, so feel free to leave a short line or two here:
www.amazon.com/review/B0C1HN8DCK
Thank you! Happy Reading,
Andrea

Made in the USA
Las Vegas, NV
17 May 2024

89968529R00125